The train lurched as it often did, and Matthew grabbed the overhead hat rack. A series of further lurches, and the train pulled into the station. Matthew retrieved his hat and strode through the door of the compartment and toward the exit. He waited impatiently for the conductor to open the door before descending to the platform.

As he had predicted, other passengers shared his desire to step off the train. He regarded the small station, but no explanation for his sense of expectancy seemed to await him there.

Several newly arriving passengers boarded other cars of the train. He turned around to study the train itself. Lights glowed from many of the windows in the various cars, even from his own compartment. He had left his curtain partially open. Nothing seemed particularly extraordinary in the presentation of the train.

The evening air in Spokane was chillier than that of Seattle, and he pulled his jacket about him more tightly. A practical man by nature, he attempted to examine the odd sensation in his breast of an erratic heartbeat. Could he be sickening? Had he assigned some metaphysical influence to what could be nothing more than the beginnings of a common cold? He hoped not. He had no time for illness and was rarely ill.

Matthew surveyed the platform one more time. Seeing nothing that would arouse curiosity much less an unusual event, he sighed heavily, returning to the train and to his compartment. He pulled open the door and froze. A woman lay on his bench seat, seemingly fast asleep, her lower limbs pulled up in a childlike pose, one hand curled under her cheek.

The roasted almond color of her hair and the dark long johns encasing her limbs marked her as the woman of his dreams.

A FALL IN TIME

BESS MCBRIDE

A FALL IN TIME

Copyright © 2014 Bess McBride

Contact information: bessmcbride@gmail.com

Cover Art by Tara West

Formatted by IRONHORSE Formatting

Published in the United States of America

ISBN: 1508961689
ISBN-13: 978-1508961680

DEDICATION

This story is dedicated to all my reader friends who enjoy the *Train Through Time* series of time travel romances.

To those of you who believe in the romance of trains, here's hoping passenger train travel continues.
There's nothing quite like it, is there?

Dear Reader,

Thank you for purchasing *A Fall in Time*. *A Fall in Time* is Book Five of the *Train Through Time series*. *A Train Through Time* was originally written as a stand-alone time travel romance, but readers asked for more, and thus a series was born.

This is Matthew Webster's story, a turn-of-the-century man who thought he lost the love of his life until he met the woman who was truly destined to become the love of his life. That she traveled 114 years through time to fall in love with him only makes it that much sweeter!

Thank you for your support over the years, friends and readers. Because of your favorable comments, I continue to strive to write the best stories I can. More romances are on the way!

You know I always enjoy hearing from you, so please feel free to contact me at bessmcbride@gmail.com, through my website at http://www.bessmcbride.com, or my blog Will Travel for Romance.

Many of you know I also write a series of short cozy mysteries under the pen name of Minnie Crockwell. Feel free to stop by my web site and learn more about the series.

Thanks for reading!

Bess

PROLOGUE

Sara Reed settled into her office chair and cracked open the window. Brilliantly lit golden leaves from the oak trees surrounding her apartment complex floated to the ground to join their brethren in mounds at the base of the trunks. A crisp breeze threatened to strip the trees of all their leaves in just that one morning. Fall had arrived.

She sipped her hot coffee and thought that nothing could improve the moment other than the sound of the train's whistle. As if on cue, the mournful, but somehow hopeful, whistle blew, and the rumbling on the nearby tracks complemented the rustling of the leaves in the trees.

Although the train's whistle blew often at regular intervals, Sara didn't always pay attention to it. But that morning, as summer ended and fall announced itself in bold colors, the whistle seemed much more poignant than usual, as if it called to her.

She eyed the open computer on her desk. She had schoolwork to do, but the scene outside her window distracted her. Another whistle of the train pulled at something inside her, demanding she interact with it. With little forethought, she clicked on Amtrak's website and pulled up the train schedule.

That she hadn't been on a train in years didn't seem to matter. The train called to her now. It was Wednesday, and she had no classes for the next few days. She had no destination in mind, no particular person who needed visiting. Something told her she needed to be on the train.

East or west? The prices made her gag. She couldn't afford to go all the way to Chicago, the eastern terminus. A train ride to Seattle, only about 300 miles away, seemed like it would end before it began. Maybe something between too short and too expensive? She chose east.

Sara studied the schedule. Unfortunately, the next train out of

Spokane heading east didn't leave until 10:30 p.m. She sighed. Hopping onto a train late at night didn't feel like it would hold the same romance as boarding during the day, but she'd take what she could get.

She closed her eyes and ran a finger along the computer screen to pick a destination. When she opened her eyes, her finger had stopped at Grand Forks, North Dakota, arriving at 11:17 p.m. the following day, a little over twenty-four hours. Why not? She had never been to Grand Forks, but the price was right, and a twenty-four-hour train trip ought to answer the call of the train. She booked a seat in coach and leaned back in her chair to look out the window again at the fall landscape.

CHAPTER ONE

Matthew Webster stowed his pocket watch in his vest and climbed aboard the train for Chicago with a heavy heart. Ten past seven in the morning. It seemed quite clear to him that Emily had decided not to see him off on his business trip this time, though that had been her habit for the past several years. There was no point in waiting any further.

With a heavy heart, he followed the porter to his compartment. The porter set his bag on the overhead compartment, and Matthew sank down onto the bench seat to stare out the window toward the station. He held out little hope that Emily would fly down the tracks, skirts whipping about her heels, hanging onto her hat with one gloved hand while she waved to him with the other.

She had given him her decision the previous day and had made it abundantly clear that she could not love him in the way that he loved her. He remembered her words.

"I *am* sorry, Matthew, but I cannot marry you. We have known each other for far too long, and I simply cannot see you as a husband. You are like a beloved brother to me." She had shaken her head sadly. "But not a husband."

Even now, Matthew felt the pain of her words. It had never occurred to them that they might not marry. Had they not always been destined for each other? Had their families not always expected it of them? Had he not always loved her—the little girl with the blonde ringlets who had lived next door, who had played hide and seek with him?

He could think of no other words to persuade her. He had told her he loved her, that he had never loved another, and then he had lowered himself to one knee and proposed. The look of shock on her face had taken him by surprise, but he had persevered.

He should have followed his instincts and stopped then. Emily's face had always been transparent, showing her every emotion. Shock was not the expression one hoped to see on the face of one's beloved when receiving a proposal.

"I can see that I have taken you by surprise, Emily," he had said. "And I must give you time to think. You know I travel to Chicago on business tomorrow. Please do not give me your final answer until you have thought about my proposal. When you come to the station to see me off in the morning, let me know if there is any hope for me."

At that moment, a maid had come to announce that visitors had arrived, and Emily excused herself with cheeks reddened by emotion.

Unwilling to imagine the rest of his life without Emily, Matthew sought to block his unknown future as he rested his head against the back of the bench seat and closed his eyes. The train pulled away, taking him away from Emily. No, that was not an apt description, not at all. The train more properly put Emily out of *his* reach.

He swallowed hard and willed himself to sleep.

He had spent a sleepless night trying *not* to concentrate on the emptiness of his future. Emily had said that they must remain friends, for hadn't they always been so? She had said she treasured their friendship and did not wish to lose it.

Then why did his future seem so bleak?

Moments later, a knock on the door startled him, and he cursed.

"Good morning, sir," the porter, a middle-aged man of African descent, said. "We are serving tea, coffee and a light breakfast in the observation lounge. Or would you like to breakfast in the dining room?"

Matthew was about to tell the porter he would dine in the dining room, but he imagined all the friendly and jovial faces he did not care to see—fellow travelers who were embarking on holidays or journeys to see family. He could not stomach the thought of so much joyful anticipation.

"Please bring me something here, will you?" he said, fishing in his wallet for a sizeable tip. "Some coffee, something to eat. I do not care what."

Matthew ignored the porter's startled look and turned away to stare out the window. The train wended its way along Seattle's waterfront as it headed north to Everett before turning east. He normally enjoyed the tranquil vista of the azure blue waters of Puget Sound, but he could take no peace from the scenery today. Even the brilliant orange and yellow foliage of the forests bordering the water could not rouse him from his despondency.

The train soon left all evidence of civilization behind with the exception of several tall ships and frigates sailing up the Sound, no doubt bound for the Pacific Ocean. Many-storied brick buildings, dusty city roads and the general haze overlying the city seemed a thing of the past.

As did his future. He sighed heavily. *Could* one's future be a thing of the past? What an odd turn of phrase, to be sure. Matthew shook his head as if to rid himself of unhelpful philosophical questions. They served only to prolong his unhappiness.

The porter returned with his breakfast, and Matthew helped himself to coffee, eyeing the food with distaste. Emily's rejection of his proposal had come after a comfortable dinner at a Seattle restaurant they had favored for several years. He had accompanied her inside her parents' house with the express request to speak to her privately.

He supposed he must consider himself lucky that he had not gone down on one knee in public. As he considered such an image, his heart thumped soundly for one quick moment as he thought that perhaps if he had... Perhaps if he had, the outcome might have been different.

He snorted. No, it was not likely. Bending on one knee in a restaurant would only serve to trip a waiter but would not have ensured that Emily agreed to marry him. No, not only agreed but eagerly anticipated such a union with him.

Matthew did not doubt that Emily loved him. Had they not been as thick as thieves for years? He also harbored no illusions that she would change her mind, that she had been mistaken in her feelings for him and could love him as a husband. Emily had been a stubborn child and had grown to become a willful, independent woman. She knew her own mind.

She did not love him as he loved her. Nothing would change that, he was certain of it.

He set down his coffee, ignored the tray of food and closed his eyes once again.

Matthew awoke some hours later with a start, somewhere in the middle of a disturbing dream. The porter must have come in and removed his tray, for it was gone. A glance out of the window showed the sky was darkening over what he knew to be vast plains of amber grass. He knew from previous travels that they must have already passed over the Cascade Mountains and were well underway toward eastern Washington.

Blearily, he retrieved his pocket watch from his vest and checked the time. Four fifty-five p.m. He had slept through the train stops in Everett and Wenatchee, and he had slept through lunch. In fact, he had mercifully slept the day away. The next stop was Spokane at approximately 7:55 p.m. Given that the weather was still mild for fall, the train, unhampered by winter snowstorms, would most likely be on time.

Matthew stood and stretched his legs, something nagging at him. Emily's image, never far from his mind these last few days, came unbidden. But it was not Emily's image that had haunted his dreams. It was not Emily's image that had awakened him so abruptly.

His dreams had centered around a young woman, a most unusual young woman. Unbound hair the color of roasted almonds danced on her shoulders. Her slender form had been encased in rather formfitting clothing that defied imagination. He could have sworn she wore nothing more on her lower limbs than thick dark underwear such as one wore on cold winter nights to bed—long johns, they were called.

Matthew pressed his lips together as he chastised himself for taking such liberties with his dreams. Women did not wear such garments, and he could not imagine how he could envision such a garment on a woman. As with most men, Matthew was no stranger to his baser side, but his parents' teachings had ensured that he regarded women with respect. He had never been one to dally the day away in sensual imaginings of women in various forms of undress.

In his estimation, a woman was infinitely more desirable if she possessed the characteristics of intelligence, humor, kindness and sound reasoning. Emily had most of those characteristics. She lacked certain elements of kindness, but he was not deterred.

Nevertheless, tightly fitting clothing aside, Matthew remembered that the young woman in his dream had sat by a window and listened to the sound of the train whistle. She sipped coffee and contemplated purchasing a ticket for the train with no particular destination in mind.

Matthew might have considered it odd to simply step aboard a train going to an undetermined location had not he been grateful for the scheduled business trip, which took him east just when he needed to leave town the most, when he felt heartsick and could not stay to see Emily day after day.

In his dreams, the young woman felt the train calling to her. That seemed a bit farfetched, but he conceded that trains held a mysterious power over him as well, and had he not needed to take the train for business, he would have traveled for the sheer joy of rumbling along on the tracks and listening for the occasional wail of the train's whistle.

The hour for dinner approached, and Matthew, knowing he must eat something, made his way to the dining car. He was seated with an elderly couple who beamed throughout the meal, stating they traveled east to attend their grandson's wedding in Chicago. Matthew nodded politely but privately wished he had asked the porter to bring him something in his compartment. The very last thing he had needed was to join people who rhapsodized about weddings and marriage.

He picked at his food and rose as soon as was polite to return to his compartment, eschewing an after-dinner drink in the observation lounge. He wanted no company, unless it was Emily's. And that was not to be.

Darkness had fallen in earnest while he was at dinner, and there was nothing to see outside the window. The porter had drawn his curtains against the night. Matthew scanned the daily newspaper but could not concentrate on the news. Tossing the paper aside, he crossed his arms and stretched out his legs as he contemplated the woman in his dreams.

Why had he not dreamed of Emily? What trick of the mind gave him the image of a strange woman to ponder? He could not remember ever dreaming of another woman. He could not actually remember dreaming of Emily either, for that matter, but never another woman. In actuality, he wasn't quite sure what he dreamed of, nor had he given it much thought.

The train's whistle blew, and he pulled aside the curtains. The lights of Spokane twinkled in the distance. A pleasant enough sight and a fine city, if about half the size of Seattle. Neither one of those things accounted for the sudden sensation of anticipation that now overcame him. He had never eagerly anticipated arrival in Spokane before unless it was his final destination, which it rarely was.

Was he meant to disembark the train and return to Seattle? Had Emily changed her mind, and he somehow simply *knew* it? Had some mystical force come to him with a message?

Matthew snorted derisively.

Again, logic and familiarity with Emily's character dictated that she had not changed her mind, and if she had, no inexplicable sense of expectation would tell him so. He pushed back the curtain and stared into the night, willing himself to calm down.

But to no avail. A restless power claimed him, and he rose to pace the compartment, keeping a sharp eye on the approaching lights of Spokane.

If nothing else, he would have to disembark from the train if only to look around, to take in some fresh air. He suspected other passengers would as well. The hour was early enough for a pleasant stroll along the station platform.

The train lurched as it often did, and Matthew grabbed the overhead hat rack. A series of further lurches, and the train pulled into the station. Matthew retrieved his hat and strode through the door of the compartment and toward the exit. He waited impatiently for the conductor to open the door before descending to the platform.

As he had predicted, other passengers shared his desire to step off the train. He regarded the small station, but no explanation for his sense of expectancy seemed to await him there.

Several newly arriving passengers boarded other cars of the train. He turned around to study the train itself. Lights glowed from many of the windows in the various cars, even from his own compartment. He had left his curtain partially open. Nothing seemed particularly extraordinary in the presentation of the train.

The evening air in Spokane was chillier than that of Seattle, and he pulled his jacket about him more tightly. A practical man by nature, he attempted to examine the odd sensation in his breast of an erratic heartbeat. Could he be sickening? Had he assigned some metaphysical influence to what could be nothing more than the beginnings of a common cold? He hoped not. He had no time for illness and was rarely ill.

Matthew surveyed the platform one more time. Seeing nothing that would arouse curiosity much less an unusual event, he sighed heavily, returning to the train and to his compartment. He pulled open the door and froze. A woman lay on his bench seat, seemingly fast asleep, her lower limbs pulled up in a childlike pose, one hand curled under her cheek.

The roasted almond color of her hair and the dark long johns encasing her limbs marked her as the woman of his dreams.

CHAPTER TWO

Sara startled awake at the sound of a sharp click, like the sound of a lock. She opened her eyes to see a tall man standing by the wooden door of some sort of room. The rumbling and swaying of the velvet bench underneath her cheek gave her no doubt that she was still on the train.

With a sharp hiss, she pushed herself upright.

"Who are *you*?" she blurted out. With one eye on the stranger, she scanned the compartment quickly. "Where am *I*?"

Sara jumped up almost as soon as she spoke. She faced off against the man who looked as stunned as she felt. Had she walked in her sleep? Did people really do that?

She remembered awakening to the sound of a clicking lock. He had locked them in together.

"Listen, I'll just get out of here, wherever here is," she said hastily with a cheesy grin. She moved toward the door, hoping he'd just step aside. So far, she'd kept her eyes from his face, thinking it best to avoid direct eye contact, which might incite him to action.

He didn't move but held a slate-gray bowler hat with the fingers of both hands. If he was going to do something, he would have to toss the hat. Sara thought she'd keep an eye on the hat. If the hat moved, then he was moving!

In her anxiety, she barely noted the luxurious furnishings of the compartment. Having never traveled in anything other than coach on a train before, she had no idea first class was so opulent. Green velvet curtains matched the forest-green upholstery on two opposing bench seats. Mahogany furniture and paneling contrasted well with the plush maroon carpet. Globed sconces provided a soft golden glow.

"Excuse me?" Sara said a little more loudly. The man rotated his hat in a circular motion, clearly agitated about something. She noted long legs encased in well-pressed dark-gray trousers. "Could you let me out?"

Still, he made no move to stand aside, and Sara was forced to either scream or look into his face. Maybe he was deaf. She opted to stall on the scream for just a minute and chose to face him.

Sara caught her breath as their eyes locked. Long dark lashes framed aquamarine eyes under dark eyebrows. Well-groomed chestnut-brown hair, slightly lighter than his eyebrows, framed a handsome, angular, clean-shaven face. His mouth was firm, the lips neither full nor thin but just about perfect, in her opinion.

Sara thought she could get lost in the blue of his eyes, now staring at her with something like shock.

"Hello?" she said, waving her hand. "Can you hear me?"

At her words, the stranger blinked and spoke.

"Who are *you*?" he asked. His voice, a deep baritone, curled her toes.

"I'm Sara Reed, but don't worry about that," she rattled. "I think I must have walked in my sleep. I'm not supposed to be here. My seat is in coach."

"I think perhaps you *are* supposed to be here, madam," he said quietly, almost in a mutter.

Sara took a step backward. This was creepy. Not yet ready to scream, she thought fast.

"No, no," she said, trying a soothing note. "My husband is waiting for me in coach. *That's* where I'm supposed to be. Soooo...if you'll just let me get by. I still don't know how I ended up here." She presumed this was his compartment. His well-tailored gray suit and matching vest suggested he had some money...or a great laundry service.

She raised her eyes to his face again and saw him search for her left hand, which she quickly tucked behind her back.

"You are married?" he asked. She didn't think his voice held disappointment so much as disbelief. Not that her marital status was any of his concern.

She still wasn't at screaming stage, but she was leaning toward it. If he made a sudden move toward her, she was prepared to bellow.

"Yes, I am," she said firmly, "and like I said, he's waiting for me. In fact, he's probably looking for me now. So, again, if you'll let me by, I'll just get out of your way and apologize for barging into your compartment. I feel a bit like Goldilocks! I promise I didn't eat the porridge." Again, she rattled nervously.

To her surprise, he moved to the side.

"I would not hold you prisoner," he said.

An odd statement, but the sentiment was what she wanted to hear.

"Good. Thanks!" Sara said. She moved toward him slowly and kept an eye on him while she fumbled with the brass lock. Even the fittings were opulent, if a little old-fashioned.

"It is not locked, madam," he said, still working his hat around in his hands.

"Oh, really?" She eyed him sheepishly. "Sorry, I thought I heard you lock the door. Okay, well, I'm off. It's nice to meet you. Thanks for your patience!"

Without waiting for his reply, Sara pushed open the heavy wooden door and stepped into the hallway. Disoriented, she wasn't sure which way to turn to get to the coach cars. Even the aisle, done in mahogany and the expensive maroon carpet, exuded luxury. Elegant globed chandeliers provided lighting, if somewhat dim.

Anxious to get away from the stranger, she quickly pulled the door shut and chose a direction. Turning right, she hurried down the corridor. Even if she went the wrong way, she could retrace her steps and stealthily pass by his compartment without detection. She resisted the urge to look over her shoulder.

She passed several more compartments before reaching the end of the car. In keeping with the rest of the décor, the door was wooden, not metal, and she grabbed the brass knob and pushed it open.

A gust of cold wind and the smell of coal assaulted her nose. Unwilling even now to turn around in case the stranger followed her, Sara pulled the door shut behind her and braced herself on the small platform between the two cars. She hadn't remembered the connector between the cars being made of a canvas-like material, but that was the last thing on her mind. She hopped across and pulled open the door of the next car, noting absently that the door had brass fittings once again, and it opened outward rather than slide as the rest of the train did.

She stepped inside and turned around to look through the window. The stranger hadn't followed her. With a sigh of relief, she turned and stopped short.

That she wasn't in the coach car was immediately apparent, but she had no idea what car she had entered. Similar to the sleeper, the walls were mahogany and the carpet luxurious. A long corridor led away on the right, but she couldn't see beyond that.

A middle-aged man of African descent who sat in a white wicker chair just inside the entrance jumped up. From his white coat, Sara assumed he was a dining car attendant. Was this the dining car?

"Hi, I'm a bit lost," she said with a shrug and an awkward smile. "I don't know how or why, but I wandered away from my seat in coach. Which way is that?"

The dining car attendant stared at her open mouthed, his dark eyes blinking as he seemed to study her yoga pants. She looked down at her legs but saw nothing to capture his interest. Her fleece jacket covered her curvier parts.

"Do you know the way? Is it that way or that way?" She pointed in both directions. "What car is this, by the way?"

"Th-the observation car, miss. I don't know about a coach car."

The door behind her opened, bringing with it the strong odor of coal she'd smelt, and Sara felt a shiver run up her spine. Without turning, she hurried past the porter and trotted down the narrow aisle to get to the next car.

A new odor assaulted her nostrils. Cigars? No one smoked on trains anymore. Was it possible Amtrak actually had a smoking room? She didn't care. She passed several closed doors and didn't pause to look in through the windows.

"Miss!" she thought she heard the porter call out, but she ignored him. Bursting into a six-foot domed room lined on both sides with wicker chairs, she gasped and stilled. Some passengers sipped hot or cold drinks and chatted with each other. Others held newspapers or books in their hands. At her entrance though, every single one of them looked up at her, and if they were talking, they stopped. It seemed as if, uniformly, they all dropped their eyes to her legs.

Sara swayed and propped a hand on a wall for support. The men were formally dressed in dark three-piece suits, high stiff white collars stretching their necks. Some wore bow ties, others elaborate neckties at the base of the collars. Almost all the men sported thick mustaches, and a few had well-groomed beards as well. The large bouffant hairdos on all of the women were a sight to behold, and Sara suspected a lot of hair supplements were used to achieve the puffy styles. High-necked blouses and jackets were topped by long skirts in varying shades from light to dark that draped over their knees and dropped to their ankles.

Sara was reminded of a favorite movie—a time travel romance in which the heroine had sported such a lovely coif and beautiful flowing skirts. It had been set in 1912. She was surprised she could remember that bit of trivia at the moment.

In a daze, she noted that the silence ended as a general buzz of conversation began, and she seemed to be at the center of it as they kept their eyes on her.

The attendant, or porter, or whoever he was, arrived on her heels.

"Miss, you can't be in here," he said urgently. She needed no further urging.

"No, I don't think I can," Sara muttered. Unable to run the gauntlet of oddly dressed people to get to the next car, she turned and darted past the porter. As she trotted back down the corridor, she slowed near several of the closed rooms that she had bypassed. Behind glass windows in the doors, she could see more well-dressed men lounging in chairs, reading newspapers and books, a drink or cup at their sides, cigars dangling from their fingers.

Where on earth was the coach car?

She hopped back across the connector and pulled open the door of the sleeping compartment. Her step quickening, she was fairly running by the time she reached the end of that car. Although she had worried the stranger would see or hear her, his door was closed, and he didn't pop his head out or grab her by the arm to drag her in.

Sara pulled open the door on the other end, the now familiar smell of coal hitting her. The next car looked no more like the modern steel train she had boarded than the last two cars, but she didn't care. She was going to find coach if it killed her, and she didn't need the help of an obviously confused car attendant.

She pushed open the door on the other side of the vestibule and stared. Opposing bench seats faced each other the length of the car. Slightly less luxurious than the first-class compartments, the furnishings were still opulent compared to the steel-framed and blue stain-proof fabric seats of the coach car she had been on. The majority of the passengers were women, all sporting the same hairstyle as the women in the other compartment. High-collared white shirts were tucked into skirts. Even from her position at the door, Sara could see ankle-length skirts peeking out from the booths.

As in the other car, wide eyes were followed by silence and then a hum of conversation, again with her at the center. Nearing panic, Sara turned and retreated to the sleeping compartment. There was only one place she could go for answers.

She ran to the stranger's compartment and beat on the door, simultaneously trying to pull it open. Now, it was locked.

"Can I come in?" she pleaded. The door opened instantly, and Sara almost fell into the room.

The stranger caught her in his arms and steadied her.

"I don't know what's happening," she whispered. "I don't know where I am. Please help me."

CHAPTER THREE

Matthew settled Mrs. Reed onto the bench. She wrung her hands together, clasping and unclasping her fingers. Her eyes looked wild, much wilder than when she had run from the compartment earlier. He had fought a hard battle with himself against following her but ultimately decided against it.

It had not been easy to let her go, knowing that he had seen her in his dreams even before he had met her. At least, he assumed so. There was always the possibility that he had absentmindedly observed her when he boarded the train, and then somehow dreamed of her, but he felt almost certain that he had not seen her before.

"Can I get you some tea or coffee, Mrs. Reed? Some water?" He reached for the door, but she put out a staying hand.

"No! Don't call the attendant," she said. She almost panted, and he grew more alarmed.

"Mrs. Reed, do you need a doctor?" he asked. He took her cold hands in his, a shock running up his arms at her touch. It was not the temperature of her hands nor the smoothness of her skin that affected him, but something else.

She shook her head and pulled her hands from his to bend over, placing her head in her lap.

"Just let me sit here a minute," she said in a muffled voice.

"Whatever are you doing, Mrs. Reed?" Matthew asked.

"I'm trying not to pass out. Surely you've seen someone put their head between their legs before, haven't you?"

"I have not, actually," he said, trying not to be shocked by her language or her actions. "Will that work?"

"I sure hope so. I haven't tried it myself before, but things are spinning, and I'm seeing black spots."

"All the more reason for you to take some refreshment, Mrs. Reed. Let me call the porter."

She lifted her head, her cheeks now flushed where they had been white pale. "The porter?" She shook her head. "I don't have any luggage."

"Luggage?" Matthew repeated. "I do not understand. I wish to call the porter to bring you something to drink and eat. Perhaps you are faint from hunger?"

"I'm so confused," she said with a shake of her head. She lowered her head to her lap again, and Matthew sat back in some confusion himself.

"Yes, I can see that you are, Mrs. Reed. How can I help you?"

"I don't know," she murmured into her lap. "Where am I?"

"You are on the train to Chicago."

"Well, that's the good news anyway."

"Good news?"

"That I'm on the train to Chicago. That's where I'm supposed to be, though I was going to get off in Grand Forks."

"Do you have family in Grand Forks, Mrs. Reed?"

She lifted her head again and regarded him.

"It's Miss Reed, or better yet, Sara. I'm not married. I lied to you about that."

Matthew opened his mouth to speak but hesitated, choosing his words carefully. He was inordinately pleased to discover there was no husband waiting for her.

"Why would you lie about that, Miss Reed?"

"I was frightened when I woke up and found you in here," she said.

He could well understand that, a single woman finding herself alone in the compartment of an unmarried man.

"I think I understand," he said carefully. "It is unusual to call a woman by her given name so early in an acquaintance. I think I must continue to call you Miss Reed."

"What's your name?" she asked. She scanned the room as if looking for something.

"Matthew Webster."

"Matthew," she repeated. He enjoyed the sound of his name on her lips but wondered why she did not more properly address him as Mr. Webster, given their short acquaintance. She was certainly a very informal young woman. However, it would be rude to correct her, and he really did not care to. Matthew it was.

She pursed her lips and blew out through her mouth before inhaling through her nose. She repeated the breathing several more times.

"Miss Reed?" he asked.

"Yes?" She turned to look at him, and he caught his breath. As he had noted earlier before she ran from the compartment, her eyes were brown with charming flecks of gold embedded in them.

"A refreshment? You must have something, or I fear you will faint."

"Water?" she asked.

"Something to eat? Did you miss dinner?"

"Noooo," she said as if uncertain. "I had dinner earlier before the train left. What time is it?"

Matthew pulled his pocket watch from his vest.

"Almost 9:00 p.m.," he said.

She stared at his watch.

"That's not possible. The train left the station at 10:30. I think I fell asleep right away."

"Ten thirty this morning? You must have slept the day away. I did as well, having had a sleepless night."

For the first time in an hour, he thought of Emily.

"No, 10:30 tonight. Wait! What day is it? I couldn't possibly have slept almost twenty-four hours."

"Wednesday," he said.

She nodded.

"Yup, it was Wednesday when I left."

"Where did you say you boarded the train?"

"Spokane."

"I fear you are quite mistaken about the departure time. It was most assuredly 7:55 p.m."

She shook her head and eyed him, almost defiantly.

"No, I don't think I'm mistaken. Are you sure that thing is working?"

She nodded toward the watch he held in his hand.

"Yes, of course my watch is working!" he said, slightly insulted. A gift from his father on his twenty-first birthday, he treasured it.

"Not too many men wear pocket watches today," she murmured, her gaze continually fixated on the watch.

Matthew looked at the watch in surprise.

"I do not know many men who do not carry a watch," he said.

She brought graceful dark eyebrows together in a frown.

"*Wear* a watch," she said as if she corrected him. "And most men just look at their phones now."

"Come now, Miss Reed! I hardly think most men even own a telephone, much less stare at it. I cannot imagine what you are talking about. You sound...disoriented."

He was trying to be kind. She looked disoriented as well, very confused. To be fair, he was experiencing his own confusion, given that he had seen her before he ever really "saw" her.

She met his eyes, and he experienced that moment of exhilaration again. His pulse quickened, and his breath stilled in his chest.

Matthew, a pragmatic man at the best of times, was not one to believe in the supernatural, but he began to wonder if such were possible, for how else had he dreamed of a woman he had never before seen but who seemed to appear out of thin air?

What force was at play here?

"I *am* disoriented," she said in a matter-of-fact voice. "But I don't think tea or coffee is going to fix it."

"Perhaps I should have the porter see if there is a doctor onboard. We do not reach our next stop in Troy, Montana, until almost 2:00 a.m. It is such a small town that I fear they might not have a doctor. Kalispell would most certainly, but we do not arrive until some time after 5:00 a.m. I am worried about you, Miss Reed."

"I'm worried about me, too," she said with a wry smile. "What are those bottles over there?"

She pointed to the glass bottles of mineral water the porter had left for his convenience.

"Water," he said. "Let me pour you a glass." He opened one of the bottles and filled a glass.

"Thank you," she murmured.

She held the glass up as if to examine the water and then took a tentative sip.

"Have you not had mineral water before?" he asked with a twitch of his lips. She really did have some unusual eccentricities, not the least of which was her clothing.

"Well, no, I don't think so. I don't think anyone really believes that bottled water comes from mineral springs." She spoke almost conversationally, although the knuckles of her hand holding the glass were white. She stared at the water as if mesmerized.

"*I* thought it did. Are you saying it does not?" he asked.

She shook her head. "No, I think it's just filtered tap water."

"Tap...as if from the water one draws in a house?"

"Yes, only on a bigger scale. In factories. Must be a pretty big filter," she said with an oddly choked chuckle.

Matthew shook his head, unwilling to argue with her over such a trivial matter. She was certainly no shrinking violet, speaking her mind as she wished.

"Is the water helping with your disorientation?" he asked. "I do believe some food would also be of benefit."

She looked up at him, her eyes shining with unshed moisture. His mouth went dry. Was she about to cry? Other than his mother on not more than one or two occasions, he had no experience with women who cried. Emily never did so, not even when they were children. She had been never been faint of heart.

He fished in his pocket for his handkerchief and held it out to her.

Miss Reed stared at the kerchief with a bemused expression before taking it.

"You know," she said in a mumble, "I'd say you're really old-fashioned, but I'm beginning to think that's not the case."

"You would be right, madam. I *am* considered old-fashioned by my friends and family. I do not aspire to many modern things and live quite comfortably in my habitual ways." He sighed and shook his head. "The turn of the century has been fraught with innumerable changes, and I prefer the older, more simpler ways. The telephone is such an invention. While my parents installed one in their house, I cannot say that I am comfortable using it. I still prefer to visit or send a note around."

He blinked as the pinkness in Miss Reed's cheeks drained away. She looked stricken, as if his words had gravely injured her in some way. What had he said?

"Miss Reed, are you all right? Perhaps you should lie down. I do not imagine there is a lady whom we could call to care for you, but I believe I might make a passable nurse." He rose hastily and pulled a pillow and blanket from the closet next to the lavatory. He placed the pillow in the corner of the bench and urged Miss Reed to lie down. She resisted, and he could not force her. She looked faint.

"What turn of the century?" she whispered.

"This year, Miss Reed, in January. Nineteen hundred."

He caught her in his arms as she slipped forward off the bench.

CHAPTER FOUR

Sara awoke to hear the rustling of paper. She dared not open her eyes for fear she would see Matthew sitting on the opposite bench in the sleeping compartment of a turn-of-the-century train. Not that she feared him exactly. And not that she feared seeing him sit across from her. No, it was the number "nineteen hundred" that had scared her. She could pretend, even to herself, that she had heard him wrong, but she hadn't. And she had known long before he said the word that something was horribly, horribly wrong.

The train rumbled on, and she heard its whistle. She was still on the train. But which one?

She slowly lifted one eyelid. As she suspected, Matthew sat on the opposite bench, his legs crossed, reading a newspaper. He had removed his jacket, revealing a formfitting gray silk vest over a crisp white shirt. He had not loosened his gray tie or the tight high collar that reached to his chin. His posture, though seemingly relaxed, was stiff and upright.

He lowered the paper to look at her before she could slam her eye shut.

"Miss Reed!" he said, dropping the paper at his side and rising to peer at her. In a motherly gesture, he laid his fingers across her forehead as if checking for a fever.

"How do you feel? You gave me quite a fright, but I think you must be exhausted. I admit to feeling guilty that I did not call for a physician, but there are elements about you, about your appearance in my compartment, that I do not wish made public. For your sake."

He allowed his fingers to trace her cheek before withdrawing his hand hastily.

Sara breathed deeply, holding back a wave of nausea. "I'm okay," she said. She pushed herself up, noting he had covered her with a blanket. She clutched the blanket to her chest and lowered her feet to the ground.

"Nineteen hundred, huh?" she said in a shaky voice. She put a hand over her mouth to stifle the queasy feeling.

He drew his brows together as if confused.

"Yes. The beginning of a new millennia."

He reached for her glass of water and handed it to her.

"Drink this. I insist. You are as pale as a ghost."

"I think I *am* a ghost," she said.

As if he couldn't help himself, Matthew's lips twitched.

"I have been contemplating *what* you are, Miss Reed, and have speculated on many supernatural notions, but I do not think you are a ghost."

Sara shook her head. "They don't burn witches anymore, do they?" she asked in a wry voice. She was trying hard not to think about the implications of what had happened to her.

Matthew's brows shot up, but he answered her gravely. "Not since the eighteenth century, Miss Reed. Do you believe you are a witch?"

She threw him a quick wide-eyed look and shook her head vehemently. No point in suggesting things to him.

"No, I was just kidding."

Matthew dropped his eyes to her legs and cleared his throat.

"May I ask you about your attire, Miss Reed? Surely you must know your...em...garments are somewhat unusual for a woman."

She looked down at her yoga pants and self-consciously pulled the blanket across her legs. Her shoes, canvas slip-ons, were probably passable, and she still wore her dark-blue fleece jacket over her red T-shirt. She had dressed for comfort, anticipating a long ride in a coach seat on a modern train, not—she found it difficult to think the words, much less say them—not travel 114 years into the past.

There! She'd said it. At some point over the past few hours, she'd accepted that she wasn't in the twenty-first century anymore. She had tried for one moment to pretend she was on a train of reenactors or had slipped into a historical movie location shoot, but she knew that was a desperate grab at any sort of rational explanation, however remote the possibility.

"My attire?" she asked, stalling as she wondered if she should tell Matthew what she thought had happened or come up with something a little more logical than the notion of time travel.

"I am quite aware that it is impolite of me to ask about your clothing, but I would not wish you to be the subject of gossip when you detrain in Grand Forks. I have never stayed in that fine town, and perhaps long johns are an accepted form of attire for the ladies, but I find that difficult to believe."

He quirked a dark eyebrow and waited for her to say something. She looked down at her lap.

"Long johns," she said in a bemused tone. She supposed they did look a bit like thermal underwear. A bit. Sara decided then and there not to tell him she thought she had traveled in time. She would "detrain" in Grand Forks and figure out something out...something. Especially a way to get back to the future.

Surreptitiously, under the blanket, she patted her jacket pockets. Empty. No wallet. No money. No phone. No, they had all been in her purse. If she had, for whatever crazy reason, actually traveled to nineteen hundred though, identification, money and a phone from the twenty-first century would do her no good. They might, in fact, get her into trouble.

"Well, yes, the long johns. I was raised by a single mother," Sara said, sticking to the truth as much as she could while lying. "Being ill a lot, she couldn't work and didn't have much money, so I wore what she could find in thrift shops. She thought these looked warm, and she bought them for me." Truthfully, her mother had bought seven pairs of baggy sweatpants that some girl must have cleaned out of her closet, and Sara had worn those in the winter throughout elementary and high school. She had longed for tight jeans like the other girls wore, but no tight blue jeans had ever shown up at the thrift store, or if they had, they'd been quickly snatched up.

Sara had been an absolute and utter geek in her hand-me-down clothing, but she hadn't realized it until she attended college on a scholarship. Few girls at Gonzaga University wore baggy sweatpants, preferring the tightly fitting yoga pants, and with her first paycheck from working in one of the school cafeterias, Sara bought several pairs. She loved them, preened in them and wore them everywhere.

Now, of course, their tightness was a bit awkward. The thought of her mother brought a knot to her throat. She had lived long enough to see Sara enter college but had died of her heart condition a year ago.

"Thrift shops?"

Sara bit her lip. Didn't they have thrift shops in nineteen hundred? How was she going to survive until she could figure out how to get back to her own time?

"Secondhand clothing stores," she explained, hoping they at least had those.

"Ah!" Matthew said. "Yes, of course." He still looked dubious, but Sara pressed her lips together in a firm smile and pulled the blanket more tightly around her.

"I have skirts at home," she said.

Matthew quirked an eyebrow.

"And where is home, Miss Reed? Are you from Spokane or Grand Forks?"

Sara quickly tried to think her answer through, but she could not reason through the implications of any particular response while Matthew watched her with those aquamarine eyes.

"Spokane," she said.

"I do not believe you ever told me if you were visiting family in Grand Forks or not," he continued.

Sara did not get the impression they were having a friendly conversation so much as she was being interrogated. And he was probably entitled to do so, since she had barged into his compartment twice, the last time asking for help.

"Yes, I'm being met by family," she said with a firm nod and what she hoped was a pleasant smile.

"I am pleased to hear that," he said. "Though I admit to some concern that you are still somewhat confused about your compartment or seat on the train."

"I beg your pardon?" Sara asked, stalling. How could she explain her desperate plea for help? "Oh, you mean when I ran into your compartment asking for help?"

He nodded. "And when I found you asleep in here only a short time before that."

"You'd think I was sleep walking or something, wouldn't you?" She really had nothing. She couldn't dazzle him with nonsense for much longer.

"Perhaps the first time you came to my compartment, but you were fully awake and quite desperate the second time you arrived."

"Yes," she conceded with a nod. She fidgeted with a corner of her blanket. Her mind was blank. If she couldn't just confess all, she had to come up with something. Anything!

"Okay, I really didn't want to have to tell you this," she began, "but..."

Nothing. Nothing!

"Yes, Miss Reed. Go on." He watched her carefully.

"Well, this is going to sound crazy," she said. Anything! *Please!*

He waited.

"I hopped aboard the train in Spokane without a ticket," she burst out. "As I told you, my mother didn't have money, and I haven't done much better."

In fact, Sara's scholarship to Gonzaga's law school, and excellent health, ensured that she would probably do much better than her mother had, but she needed some excuse for not having a ticket.

Matthew reared his head at her words as if they surprised him.

"I *did* want to go visit family in Grand Forks," she hurried on to say. "My grandmother is ill. And since I didn't have any money, I snuck onboard the train. Please don't tell them. They'd only throw me off." She clasped her hands in front of her. She was serious about that part.

The furrows on Matthew's forehead relaxed, and his eyes softened. Sara felt awful lying to him, but she didn't see that she had any alternative.

"I apologize, Miss Reed. It was most uncharitable of me to force you into such an embarrassing confession. No, of course I will not reveal your secret to the conductor or porter, and you are free to use my compartment as long as need be. I shall make arrangements for another compartment." He rose, picked up his hat and reached for an overcoat and a small bag in an overhead bin.

"No, wait!" Sara jumped up. "Don't do that! I don't want you to have to move."

He blinked, and she realized he really had no choice, not if this was really nineteen hundred.

"But we cannot stay in the same compartment, Miss Reed."

"But if you ask for another compartment, they'll want to know why, and they'll know I'm here. They will want me to pay, and I don't have any money." All of this was true at least, though somehow the truth wasn't making her feel any better.

Matthew stilled, appearing to give the matter some thought.

"Yes, I do see your point, Miss Reed." He pressed his lips together and looked toward the door. "I think it best I pay for your fare and compartment to Grand Forks." He held up a hand when Sara opened her mouth to object. "I insist. It is not a problem, nor do I think the conductor will object too strenuously. He may consider it irregular, but the company will be handsomely recompensed."

He moved to the doorway but turned back.

"Sleep well, Miss Reed. The porter will turn down the bed and bring you coffee in the morning. Perhaps we could have breakfast together?"

Sara, dumbfounded at his rather generous offer, nodded.

"I don't know what to say. Thank you."

He inclined his head.

"Not at all," he said. "Shall I instruct the porter to awaken you at seven o'clock?"

Sara nodded again.

"Very well. I will pick you up at 7:30 for breakfast. Good night, Miss

Reed. Lock the door behind me. Open it only for the porter."

He stepped out, and Sara moved to the door and locked it. Her legs, shaking as they had been, gave out, and she sagged against the door.

What on earth had happened to her? How could she possibly have awakened from a short doze to find herself on a train in nineteen hundred? The last thing she remembered was sitting in her seat reading a book. She'd been so sleepy though, having gotten up early for work at the cafeteria, that she must have fallen asleep almost as soon as the train left the station.

She didn't need to see proof that she was in another time. Matthew was proof. His clothing, the immaculate styling of his hair with a cute little part on the side, the longish sideburns, even the derby he carried with him. And if Matthew wasn't proof, the men and women she'd seen in the other car told her that unless she was on a film set and no one had yelled "cut" at her presence, then she had traveled in time.

She remembered the sensation of the train's whistle "calling" to her—the reason she had booked the trip. She never expected though that the train, rather than take her east, would drag her back in time to the turn of the twentieth century. She had no affinity for nineteen hundred that she could think of, no dreams of living in the past other than a redo of her elementary and high school years. She had no ancestors she thought she needed to visit, no wrongs to rectify, and no particular historical expertise in the era.

If anything, she would have traveled only far enough into the past to know her mother as a child, before her congenital heart defect made her life difficult. But certainly not over one hundred years.

Why had this happened to her? Had it happened to others? Did other people travel through time? Why hadn't she heard anything about it before?

Sara's knees buckled, and she slumped to the floor, pulling her knees to her chest. Had she lost her mind? Had she gone crazy? Perhaps her mother's early death had driven her over the edge—always a possibility.

She stared down at her black yoga pants and pulled at the stretchy material, letting it snap back against her leg. She repeated the motion. What on earth was she going to do in Grand Forks, North Dakota? It was early November. Snow would definitely be setting in soon, if it hadn't already. The nights were already cool in Spokane. For that matter, what would she do in Spokane in nineteen hundred?

CHAPTER FIVE

"No, sir, I'm sorry, but we have no empty first-class sleeping compartments. All are spoken for. Is there a problem with your compartment?" the conductor asked.

Matthew regarded the tall, thin, middle-aged man. A generous gray mustache dominated his face. Pale blue eyes watched him curiously.

"No, not at all. Unbeknownst to me, my...sister came aboard the train in Spokane as a surprise. I did not realize she was on the train until we left. But she is onboard, and I must pay her fare. I am certain you understand."

Even to Matthew's ears, his story sounded unlikely. He composed his face into a grave expression and stared at the conductor.

"That is very irregular, sir. You must know from your frequent travels that stowing away is not permissible, Mr. Webster."

Matthew stiffened, unused to be addressed in such a tone, but he thought better of a retort and opted to accept the censure.

"Yes, I know, Conductor, and I have chastised my sister for her ill-conceived prank. You do understand though why I need another compartment."

"Are you unwilling to share your compartment with your sister, sir? There are two berths in that compartment."

Matthew's face blanched, and he drew in a sharp breath. "I...I think she must have her privacy."

"The train is very full this evening, Mr. Webster. Almost all the seats have been reserved on the train, even those in the tourist sleeper. There is one bed available, but only one, and it is in tourist class."

Matthew had never ridden in the tourist class in his life, but it seemed he had no other option.

"Yes, that will do nicely. Thank you. Could you direct me to the tourist car?"

Not only had he never ridden in tourist class, he had never even seen the car.

"They will be turning the berths down now, sir, so we should hurry."

"Yes, thank you. Would you ensure that the porter awakens my sister at seven o'clock for breakfast?"

"Yes, of course," the conductor said. He led the way through several cars, including the dining car, until they reached the tourist sleeper. A porter, standing on a small footstool in the narrow aisle, looked up as they entered.

"George, Mr. Webster is going to take berth fifteen."

"Yes, sir," said the porter, a small, wiry, middle-aged man. He jumped down from his stool. "This way, sir."

"I hope you'll be comfortable, Mr. Webster," the conductor said with a dubious quirk of a gray eyebrow.

"I am certain I will be very cozy, Conductor. Thank you."

Matthew privately wondered how he could manage, but he steeled himself. If he had worried about sleeping in the compartment with Miss Reed before, from all appearances, he was about to sleep with several women. Men and women were interspersed throughout the tourist sleeping car with no thought to gender, other than that they did not seem to share the same berth.

He had a distinct impression of green—green carpets, green curtains, green cushions on the high-backed benches on the right side of the train, those not yet converted to beds. All furnishings appeared to share a similar degree of luxury that the first-class sleeper enjoyed. All that was lacking was space and privacy.

Matthew followed George down the aisle, trying to avoid glancing into the small curtained alcoves that appeared to be no more than two stacked bunks behind a curtain. Where did the passengers change clothing before retiring? Where did they wash up? Shave?

"Here you go, sir," the porter said. He pulled aside a curtain, revealing two Spartan berths, the upper bunk suspended from the concave walls of the car by sturdy-appearing chains.

A rather large gentleman perched on the edge of the bottom bunk, his girth suggesting he might have difficulty fitting into the narrow space. Indeed, even now, his face reddened as he attempted to swing his legs up onto his bed. The porter rushed to help, and the gentleman was safely deposited into his small alcove in a reclining position.

"Good evening," Matthew said politely, though he doubted his own wishes.

"Evening," the gentleman huffed. He nodded briefly, his graying beard bobbing once, before pulling a thick woolen blanket over his shoulder and turning away onto his side.

Matthew eyed the upper berth, resembling something like a shelf. Two small pillows encased in white linen perched at the head—or foot—of a narrow, lumpy-appearing mattress, stored as it normally was against the overhead bulk.

"And how might I ascend to that lofty position?" he asked George.

"Here's a ladder, sir," George said, positioning a wooden ladder against the bunk.

"And where could I wash up?"

"There's a dressing room, washroom and toilet down the hall, sir," he said.

Matthew nodded and set his small bag on top of his bunk. He could do little to avoid disturbing his berth companion, but it seemed as if that worthy gentleman had already succumbed to sleep, for a rumbling snore could be heard.

"Will there be anything else, sir?" George asked, his eyes darting around the car as if to ascertain what or who else needed his attention.

"No, thank you, George." Matthew nodded and opened his bag to retrieve his nightclothes, a dressing gown, slippers and his toiletries. He made his way down to the dressing room and changed into his pajamas, dressing gown and slippers before stepping into the tiny washroom to perform the necessaries.

He stared at his reflection in the mirror with bemusement, wondering how exactly he found himself in a very public tourist car without the usual degree of privacy he expected when he traveled. Was he simply to traverse the aisle in his red silk dressing gown for the world to see?

Still, he could not have imagined Miss Reed in his position. Her clothing alone would have elicited shocked regard, if not comment.

He returned to his berth only to discover that a tall gentleman, assisting his equally tall wife into an upper berth, had appropriated the ladder. The porter had vanished.

Matthew set his clothing and toiletries on his bunk and waited patiently. The gentleman did not return the ladder but climbed into his own bed and pulled the curtain.

With a sigh of what he considered to be infinite patience, Matthew reacquired the ladder and climbed into his berth. He stored his clothing and toiletries inside his case and stowed the whole onto a small rack provided.

He drew the curtain shut, lowered himself down onto the mattress to lie on his back, and pulled the blanket up to his chest. His companion snored without relief, as did several other passengers from the sound of the symphony echoing throughout the car.

The train rumbled along the tracks, the normal swaying of the car now intensified by the elevated position of his bed. He hoped he wouldn't fall out of the bunk. There was no barrier to prevent it.

Sleep seemed highly unlikely. The combination of the noise of his sleeping companions, uncertainty about his precarious position on the upper berth, and questions about Miss Reed could only serve to thwart a good night's rest.

Where on earth was the woman really from? Miss Reed was different from any young lady he had ever known, and now that he was apart from her, distanced from the beseeching look in her brown eyes, he found he could not truly believe her tale of stowing away on the train to visit a sick grandmother in North Dakota. Perhaps some elements of her story were true, but in general, the premise for her predicament smacked of fiction.

Matthew thought Miss Reed must indeed be destitute, and he had no doubt that she did need help, but he was unsure what he could do for her other than what he already had. He would have to wait until they reached Grand Forks to assuage his curiosity. He knew from experience that the train would not reach Grand Forks until approximately eleven o'clock the next morning. Until then, he must satisfy himself that she had a comfortable bed and food in her stomach.

He realized that he had not thought of Emily over the past few hours as much as he thought he might. He had thought his journey, close on the heels of her rejection, might be excruciatingly long and tedious, given his misery, but it seemed as if Miss Reed's mysterious appearance and predicament had forestalled his despondency, an unexpected state of affairs for which he must be grateful.

Emily, adventurous even as a child, would have enjoyed the mystery that was Miss Reed. She would have had little qualm in delving deeper into Miss Reed's story—questioning and probing even to the point of rudeness. Emily's parents had been indulgent, rarely attempting to constrain their only child. Matthew's parents, though quietly decrying the amount of freedom Emily enjoyed, said nothing, knowing their only son was besotted with his next-door neighbor and childhood playmate.

Though he had informed his parents he would soon be asking for Emily's hand in marriage, he had not the heart to tell them she had rejected him. There had been little time at any rate, as that was not the sort of information one simply left in a note, and his early train departure prevented him from seeing them in person that morning.

But Emily would never know Miss Reed, would never know the

mystery he now encountered. Their friendship was forever altered by his proposal and her rejection, and he wondered if he would ever feel comfortable confiding in her again. It was to Emily he had told most of his secrets, save one. He had not told her of his dream to be married to her, to have a family and a home of his own. Though he could well afford to maintain his own house, he still resided in the Webster family residence in Seattle until such time as he married.

He realized now, too late, that Emily had never discussed marriage, or children either. It seemed that all the ladies of his acquaintance spoke of the virtues of the married state and motherhood, and if unmarried, young women had not hidden their desire to become brides.

How was it that he and Emily had never discussed the matter before? He sighed heavily. He knew only a portion of the answer. For his part, he had assumed marriage with Emily to be a certainty, the natural course of his life. Blindly, he saw now, he had never thought to question his beliefs.

The jostling of the train finally lulled him to sleep. It was not Emily's face that haunted his dreams though, but the words Miss Reed had echoed when she returned to his compartment.

"I don't know what's happening," she had whispered with a stricken expression. "I don't know where I am. Please help me."

CHAPTER SIX

Sara awakened to the sound of the train slowing. She pushed aside the blanket and peeked out the window of the train. Still dark, she had no idea what time it was. The train lurched, screeched, and a loud burst of steam hissed as it came to a stop in front of a station.

Kalispell, Montana, the sign over the rather large two-story building showed. From the lamps glowing on either side of the station door, Sara could tell the building was brick.

A group of passengers waited under the light of lampposts to board the train. If she had ever hoped to awaken from a dream, those hopes were well and truly gone. The men dressed in suits and derbies, with the occasional cowboy hat interspersed throughout, and the women wore long skirts and broad-brimmed hats.

A commotion in the hallway galvanized her into action. Without thinking, Sara shoved her feet into her shoes, shrugged on her jacket and opened her door. Passengers nodded as they passed her, intent on following the porter to their compartments. As soon as they passed, she turned right and hurried for the exit. Finding it not in the middle as she expected, she trotted toward an open door at the end of the car.

An unexpected blast of cold air hit her in the face as she stepped out onto a platform. In the darkness, she had missed the patches of snow along the tracks and around the edge of the train depot.

She hurriedly descended a set of steep metal stairs and hopped onto a wooden platform. The activity at the station, given the darkness, surprised her. Porters and luggage handlers rushed around, carrying cases back and forth. Wagons with horses waited patiently while goods were transferred from the train to the wagons or vice versa. A clock showed it was about seven minutes to six—she assumed in the morning.

She turned to look back toward the train. The conductor walked the platform, ushering passengers aboard. Hidden as she was by the bustle on the platform, he didn't pay attention to her.

The train itself wasn't the sleek silver train she had boarded in Chicago but something straight out of a vintage train photograph. A large black locomotive spouted steam and was followed by a long line of dark coaches, looking a lot like forest-green Pullman cars. Great Northern was painted across the front of each one of them.

Sara regretted her impulsive decision to get off the train. She realized now that she might not be able to reboard the train without a ticket. There was no way she could just sneak on. A porter stood by the door, helping passengers aboard, but he wasn't the porter who had turned down the bed in Matthew's compartment.

She wasn't sure what had driven her to jump off the train. A desire to escape the nightmare in which she now found herself? As if by hopping down from the train, she would find herself back in her own time? Or maybe she didn't know what she was going to do in Grand Forks, North Dakota. Her original plan had been to stay the night near the station and return to Spokane the following day, her crazy itch for train travel scratched. But she had no better way to get back on the train in Grand Forks than she had here in Kalispell, Montana.

A shiver took hold of her, and she eyed the doorway to the sleeper car. The last of the passengers had boarded, and the porter disappeared. A burley man pushing a cart stopped and climbed aboard to deposit what looked like stacks of newspapers just inside the doorway before descending and moving down to the next car.

Since Matthew Webster had kindly given her his compartment, Sara knew she was better off on the train than not, no matter where it went. At least she was warm and had a bed to sleep in until she reached Grand Forks. She approached the stairs with caution but froze when the porter, the one she didn't know, reappeared in the doorway to pick up the newspapers.

No, she wasn't going to be able to get back on. She could attempt to lie, saying she'd forgotten her ticket in her compartment, but it was unlikely he would believe her, given her clothing. She was fully aware that she didn't look like the other women who had boarded the train.

She watched the porter sort through the papers, hoping he would disappear again. She hoped the other porter would come by and that he would recognize her as a passenger. She supposed she could invoke Matthew's name, but she couldn't remember his last name. The visual of her stating that some tall, handsome guy named Matthew let her sleep in his compartment since she didn't have a ticket stumped her. No, that wasn't going to work.

"All aboard!" the conductor called out from his position further down the line of cars. Sara gasped. She had to get aboard. Why, oh why had she gotten off the train?

She dashed for the stairs just as the porter shut the door. Stopping short, she looked to her right to see the conductor climbing aboard as the train began to move. Short of jumping from the platform and clinging to the stairs, Sara could do nothing but watch it leave.

The bustle at the train station did not end with the train's departure, but time seemed to stand still for Sara. As if flaunting its warmth and relative security, the lights of the train twinkled as it disappeared around a bend.

Sara swallowed hard against the lump in her throat. Crying wasn't going to help her predicament. She turned around and studied the station again. What was she going to do? Probably the same thing she would have done in Grand Forks, North Dakota, but what?

She caught the occasional glances of workers, but in general, they seemed to be a busy group, probably in a hurry to complete their tasks and climb back in bed. She eyed the station but thought it best to avoid it, at least for the moment. A shiver overtook her again, and she wondered how she was going to manage. She tried hard not to think about the future. This aberration of time and place couldn't last forever. It just couldn't.

"Look out there!" a man yelled, and Sara looked over her shoulder. A man with a cart of luggage attempted to go around her, but she stepped out of his way.

She couldn't just stand on the platform, especially once the sun came up. She eyed several wooden benches positioned along the brick wall. No one huddled on them, so she guessed she wouldn't be huddling there either. She would surely be chased away. And to what end would she perch on a bench? She couldn't very well live at the train station, wishing and hoping she would somehow be transported forward in time.

Or could she?

Sara changed her mind and made her way into the depot building. She stepped inside the doorway and scanned the interior. Some passengers still congregated as if awaiting luggage and rides. A station agent stood behind a counter, helping out other passengers.

A stairwell led off to the right, and Sara headed for that without looking over her shoulder. If someone yelled, she would stop, but until then, she was going to move fast. She hurried up the wooden stairs and reached the second floor, a long carpeted hallway flanked by a series of closed doors. She started twisting knobs and looking in, noting offices that looked as if they might be in use during the day. None of the rooms appeared unused.

She leaned against the final door and sighed. Not even a bathroom. That must be located on the first floor. Could she find a storage room or something on the first floor? Where did they store parcels and packages? Surely they had a room for abandoned luggage?

Sara crept back down the stairs and hugged the wall. Luckily, the station agent looked too occupied to notice her. She peered around the edge of the stairs. Packages and boxes were stacked along the wall just to her right, as if waiting to be stored. She took a deep breath and darted out of the relative darkness of the stairwell and around the corner. She pushed open the door behind the packages and jumped into a darkened room.

Sara dared not flip on a light switch even if she thought she could find it. She eased the door shut behind her and paused, waiting for her eyes to adjust to the dim light. Several windows allowed reflected light from the lamps outside the building to dispel some of the darkness.

The room definitely appeared to be for storage. Packages and boxes were stacked on wooden shelves. Several pieces of old-fashioned luggage were piled into a corner to the left of the door.

It was likely the station agent or baggage handlers would enter the storeroom to store more boxes and packages once the crowd from the train thinned. She didn't see how she could escape detection in here for long.

Sara eyed the luggage. Abandoned? Maybe she could at least find a warmer coat in one of the cases.

Sara pressed a button on one of the locks on the smallest case, a little square thing. Unlocked, it popped open. She closed it again and, thinking the case would be light, was surprised to discover that she had to half carry, half drag the luggage to the far corner of the large room. Had she known the bag would be so heavy, she would have grabbed one of the larger cases.

She found a secluded spot behind a large shelf holding boxes and set the case down. The light coming through the window shone on the brass fittings of the case, and she fumbled with the locks again.

The case opened, and she quietly eased the sides down to the floor to study the contents. Sara wasn't about to say that luck favored her, because she was pretty sure it hadn't, but the case did appear to belong to a woman—a woman who was going to lose some of her clothing, if she hadn't abandoned her luggage.

Sara squinted and pulled out a long dark garment—a skirt, though she couldn't really make out the color. The material felt like cotton.

Fascinated, she rummaged further and found a light-colored, long-sleeved blouse, also in cotton. What else would she need? Something to keep her warm. Shoes? She felt her way among the things in the case, touching something hard. She pulled a pair of ankle boots from the case and held them up to her feet. They seemed a bit large, but she decided to take them anyway.

By now, a sliver of daylight lightened the sky outside, making it easier to see the contents of the case, but also making discovery easier by anyone who came into the room and walked toward the back.

She jumped to her feet, stepped out of her canvas shoes and pulled the skirt over her yoga pants. If anything, the pants would actually serve as long johns, keeping her warm underneath the skirt.

The skirt fit snugly around her waist, a large band coming to a point over her abdomen. She slipped out of her red T-shirt and into the long-sleeved blouse. Unfortunately, the high-necked blouse appeared to button down the back, and she could only reach the buttons at her neck. No matter, she had no intention of giving up her warm fleece jacket.

There appeared to be an excessive amount of material on the front of the blouse, and she wondered if that was the style. Sara ran her hands across her neck and upper chest to feel intricately crocheted lace.

She shrugged and bent to slip her foot into one of the boots. Scratchy on the inside, she quickly pulled it off. No, her own shoes would have to do, just like the fleece jacket. Surely they had eccentric dressers in nineteen hundred, didn't they?

She glanced out the window again to see that she was probably now visible to anyone outside, and she ducked down. She'd have to get out of the storeroom for now, perhaps for the day, but it might be a place to sleep at night, at least until she could figure out what to do with herself.

Sara secured the case and returned it to its place. She hoped the owner of the case wouldn't recognize the clothes Sara wore. She grabbed her T-shirt and eyed it. What to do with the bright thing?

She folded it as flat as she could and lifted her skirt to tie it around her hips. Then she shrugged into her jacket, noting she couldn't zip it up, given the fullness of the lace on the front of the blouse. She shrugged and moved to the door. The station had quieted somewhat, and Sara eased the door open.

All the passengers had dispersed, and the lobby was empty. She scanned the counter on the opposite side of the room but didn't see the station agent. She pulled the door wide enough to slip through and popped outside, closing the door behind her without turning around.

She moved along the wall, trying to appear invisible as she headed for the front door. A large sheet of paper on a bulletin board caught her eye—Help Wanted!

She looked over her shoulder, and seeing no one about, took time to read the notice.

"Help Wanted! Ticket Clerk. Must be able to read and write English. Please inquire at the counter."

Sara drew in a sharp breath. Well, she could certainly read and write English. She looked down at her clothing. The lights of the lobby revealed that her bell-shaped skirt was dark blue, the blouse a soft white. She pulled the sides of her jacket tightly across her chest and turned to stare at the counter. How hard could it be? She needed a job, especially if she was to find somewhere to stay. She had no idea how long she was stuck in nineteen hundred, but she didn't think she could stay in the train station without being discovered.

The door leading to the platform opened, and a tall man stepped in. Sara's heart thumped. Outlined against the gray light of dawn, he looked like Matthew!

"Can I help you, miss?" the man said, removing a conductor-style hat. The lights shown on his face. No, not Matthew. His hair was white, and he was considerably older, maybe in his early sixties. He was the station agent she had seen behind the counter.

He approached, and Sara held her breath, certain she couldn't pass for a turn-of-the-century woman. Her knees shook under the skirt.

"Miss?" he asked.

"I was wondering about the job," Sara blurted out.

The agent's thick white handlebar mustache twitched as if he hadn't heard right. He blinked.

"The ticket clerk?" he asked.

Sara nodded. "I can read and write English."

"Yes, I'm sure you can," he said, fixing her with amused blue eyes, "but I can't say that we've ever hired a woman for the job."

Sara stiffened.

"Well, it's a good time to start, don't you think?" she asked. "I'm new in town, and I need a job. I promise you, I can do the job if you show me how."

"Where are you from, Miss..."

"Sara Reed." She thrust out what she hoped was a businesslike hand. He shook it.

"I'm from Spokane," she finished. She wanted to smile, but her face seemed frozen.

"Walter Wheeler," he said. "I suppose you're right. I know other stations have hired a few women as telegraphers and clerks. I guess we could too."

35

He raised a hand to twirl a corner of his mustache as if he was thinking. Sara begged him silently but kept her face immobile while she waited.

"Tell you what. You sound like a smart girl. Let's try you out for a few days. If you don't get it, no harm. Whaddya say?"

Sara breathed a sigh of relief.

"Great!" she said. "When do I start?"

He turned and looked at the counter. "Well, you could start right now. I've got some time to show you the ropes. We're not too busy right now."

Sara resisted the temptation to stall. She was hungry, tired and, frankly, scared, but she needed the job. Walter was likely to tell her to take a hike if she came up with any reason why she couldn't start right away.

"Sounds good," she said. She followed him around the perimeter of the counter and through a door leading into the agent's office.

For the next few hours, Sara ignored her hunger pangs as she watched and listened to Walter. Though she warmed up, she kept her jacket on, remembering that her blouse was only half buttoned down the back. She also ignored her need to use the restroom—Walter apparently requiring no such breaks.

Almost three hours after they started, Walter leaned back in his wooden office chair.

"I think you're catching onto this stuff pretty quickly," he said. "How about a break for lunch? I don't suppose you brought any food with you."

Sara, pressing her legs tightly together, shook her head. She licked her parched lips.

"I need to use the restroom," she said.

Walter nodded in the direction of a door that sported the sign Toilet.

"Thanks," she said. She stood, pushed back her chair and promptly tripped over her skirt. Walter jumped up and caught her.

"Steady there, young lady," he said with a laugh.

With a red face, Sara thanked him, and clutching her skirt, she headed for the bathroom. She stepped inside and looked around. Not an unpleasant room, the floor was tiled in white and the single porcelain sink clean. The toilet was different—but not so unusual that she couldn't figure out the need to pull the chain to make it flush.

She did her best to simultaneously wriggle her yoga pants down while hiking the snug bell-shaped skirt as high as she could. She managed successfully, and business concluded, she pulled the chain to hear a gurgle of water. She moved to the sink and washed her hands, drying them on the available cotton towel.

The single mirror over the sink reflected her image from the chest up, and she bent forward to eye the lovely lacework on her blouse. Something seemed off, and Sara tilted her head and looked at her face. Dark shadows highlighted the darkness of her brown eyes. Her skin looked pale against the brunette tones of her shoulder-length hair, which now looked tousled.

Her hair! No! Women didn't wear their hair willy-nilly at the turn of the century, did they? No! They wore it up in buns. What must Walter have thought of her?

Sara turned and surveyed the room, looking for a length of string or twine or something, but the room was fairly Spartan. Her hair was fine and just a little curly. There was no way she was going to be able to just wrap it up into a bun and have it stay.

Her T-shirt! Sara lifted her skirt again and pulled the T-shirt from around her waist. She bit and tugged and pulled until she managed to tear off a length of the bright-red hem. She tied the now shredded T-shirt around her waist again, and eyed her hair.

Pulling it up to the crown of her head, she wrapped the T-shirt ribbon around her hair in a ponytail. Then she wrapped the whole into a bun, securing it within the confines of the ribbon.

She tried twisting this way and that but couldn't see her handiwork in the mirror. All she could do was hope that it passed for presentable.

She returned to the office to find Walter on his feet and waiting for her.

"Let's go have some lunch at the café," he said, donning his hat.

Sara balked.

"I...uh...I'm not hungry," she said. She was starving, but she had no way to pay for lunch. She'd been so busy trying to learn the job, she hadn't yet figured out how she was going to eat...or sleep.

"Sure you are! My treat," he said. He held the door of the office open.

Sara didn't argue. If this was going to be her last meal for a while, she'd take the freebie! She followed Walter out of the station and into the rest of the early twentieth century.

CHAPTER SEVEN

Matthew awakened to a jolt of the train, momentarily disoriented to time and place. He turned toward the window to ascertain the approximate time of day but could find no window. A dark curtain across the length of his bed to the right confused him.

The train! The tourist sleeper! Yes, he was in the tourist sleeper. He pushed himself upright and pulled aside the velvet curtain. Light flooded the compartment from the now unshaded windows of several of the lower berths. He peered over the edge of his berth to find that his companion had risen and vanished, the bed still unmade.

Several people moved to and fro in the aisle, some fully dressed, some in dressing gowns. Matthew reached for his vest to retrieve his pocket watch.

Five minutes before seven. He could not remember whether he had instructed the porter to awaken him, but he had asked the conductor to ensure that Miss Reed was awakened at seven for breakfast. He was to pick her up at 7:30.

Matthew, eschewing a ladder, grabbed his clothing and toiletries and swung his legs over the edge of the upper berth to lower himself to the ground. He fumbled for his dressing gown and slippers and slipped those on before hurrying off to the dressing room.

Accomplishing the necessaries in good time, with case in hand he retraced his steps to the first-class sleeping compartment. As he approached the compartment, his heart began to thump uncomfortably against his chest, and he attributed the sensation to renewed concern for Miss Reed and her plight. The train was due to reach Grand Forks late that night, and he truly hoped that family awaited her at the station. If they did not, he was not certain he could allow Miss Reed to detrain.

He quirked an eyebrow at his own audacity. It was not, of course, within his power to prevent her from leaving the train, but he thought he might attempt to dissuade her from doing so if she was without family or means. He hoped he might have opportunity to delve further into her history during the course of the day.

However, at the moment, he planned to leave his case in the first-class sleeping compartment and escort Miss Reed to breakfast. He knocked on the compartment door and waited.

When she failed to answer, he knocked again. Another check of his watch showed him it was 7:30 on the dot. He prided himself on his punctuality.

"Miss Reed?" he called in a low voice. He knocked again.

No response.

Matthew pulled the door slightly ajar but turned his head in case Miss Reed was not yet dressed.

"Miss Reed, are you in there?"

Still no response. He turned and pulled the door wide. The compartment appeared to be empty. The bed was made, and there was no sign of Miss Reed. He knocked on the door of the lavatory, but she didn't respond.

"Good morning, sir," the porter said as he stepped into the room with a tray holding coffee service.

Matthew swung around.

"George! Where is Miss Reed, the lady—my sister, who is staying in here?"

"I don't know, sir. She was gone when I came to wake her. I thought she might have gone into breakfast."

"Yes, that's it!" Matthew said hastily. He dropped his case on the bench seat. "I'll find her there."

He hurried past the porter and made his way to the dining car. A check of the diners failed to reveal Miss Reed. Where could she be?

Matthew made a thorough search of as many of the cars as possible, but Miss Reed was not among the passengers. He returned to his compartment, hoping to find her there, but she had not returned to the room in his absence.

He dropped to the bench seat and stared out the window.

George stopped by again.

"Can I get you anything, sir? Coffee, tea?"

Matthew turned to regard the porter.

"Are you certain you didn't waken Miss Reed, that is...my sister, this morning, George? Did you see her at all? Anywhere on the train?"

George shook his head. "No, sir, I haven't seen her this morning. The last time I saw her was when I turned the bed down last night."

Matthew pressed his lips together. What Miss Reed did was really no concern of his, but he could not help but worry.

"Please ask the conductor if I could see him, George."

"Right away, sir."

Matthew alternately sat and stared out the window or stood and paced the floor. He was pacing when the conductor arrived.

"You asked to see me, Mr. Webster?"

Matthew, intent on counting the flowered pattern in the carpet, looked up.

"Yes, thank you for coming. My...sister has gone missing. Have you seen her? I was supposed to meet her here for breakfast at 7:30." Matthew pulled his watch from his vest as he had done many times in the past hour.

The conductor shook his head. "No, sir, I haven't seen her. Did you check the dining room?"

Matthew nodded impatiently. "And every other car. I cannot find her anywhere. I have to say that I am growing worried."

"I am afraid I never saw her, Mr. Webster, so I wouldn't recognize her if I did. Is it possible that she got off the train in Troy or Kalispell?"

Matthew drew in a sharp breath and stared hard at the conductor.

"Surely, someone would have seen her. What time did we arrive in Troy?"

"Around 2:00 a.m. And we left Kalispell on time at 5:55 a.m."

Matthew checked his watch again. Eight-twenty.

Had Miss Reed left the train at Troy or Kalispell? Why? Both towns were in Montana, quite a distance from Grand Forks, North Dakota.

What if some terrible fate had befallen her? An accident? Kidnapping? Something worse?

"Please send a telegraph to those stations at your earliest convenience to see if she left the train," Matthew said. "I find it difficult to believe that my sister would leave the train voluntarily." He had done his utmost to ensure that Miss Reed was in comfortable circumstances. Why would she leave the train?

"Of course, Mr. Webster. We won't reach Havre, Montana, until this afternoon at 3:20, and I won't be able to send a telegram until then. Additionally, we won't be able to wait for an answer. I can direct a response to the Glasgow station, but we won't get arrive at that station until 7:45 tonight."

Matthew turned away impatiently.

"That is much too late!" he barked. "I am very concerned about her disappearance."

"I understand, sir, but there is little I can do at the moment."

Matthew took a deep breath. His hands were cold, and his heartbeat alternately raced uncomfortably. A knot gnawed in the pit of his stomach. He truly hoped no harm had befallen Miss Reed.

"Yes, thank you, Conductor. I understand."

"I will need your sister's description."

"Petite, tiny, disheveled shining brown hair hanging about her shoulders, gold-flecked brown eyes. She wore a dark-blue jacket and black trousers that resemble long johns."

The conductor regarded him with raised brows. "A thorough description. And her name again?"

"Miss Sara Reed," Matthew said. "She is my half sister," he improvised.

"Yes, sir. Of course."

"As soon as we reach Havre," Matthew said.

"Yes, sir," the conductor said again. With a tip of his cap, he left the compartment.

Matthew spent the next few hours pacing his compartment and wandering from car to car, still searching for Miss Reed. He paused long enough to order and eat a sandwich in his compartment and then resumed his travels. The newspaper, normally an interesting diversion, was tedious at best, and he returned to his contemplation of the passing scenery...and wondering about Miss Reed's whereabouts.

George came to remove his luncheon plate and left the compartment without a word.

Matthew sighed heavily. He rested one arm on the windowsill and tapped it restlessly. He was fully aware that his concern over a stranger was bordering on obsession, but there seemed little he could do to assuage his anxiety. That he had dreamed of her before meeting her must have meant something, but he could not know what.

Had he been able to speak to Emily regarding the mysterious appearance and disappearance of Miss Reed, he might have felt better. Emily, his closest confidant since childhood, would no doubt have put the entire matter into perspective, but he found himself unable to contemplate the situation with any degree of logic.

At long last, the train slowed for arrival in Havre. Matthew rose and sought out the conductor. The conductor, busy with detraining passengers, saw him and nodded.

"I haven't forgotten, Mr. Webster."

"No, of course not. How long are we at the station? I wondered if we might not get a response while we are here."

"We're only here for twenty minutes, sir. Barely enough time to send the telegrams, much less receive one."

"Yes, I see. Well, anything is possible," Matthew said. Knowing himself to be a nuisance, he ignored the unusual sensation and followed the conductor into the station.

Foolishly, while he waited for the conductor to talk to the station agent, Matthew found himself looking for Miss Reed in the crowd, but to no avail. She was not there.

The conductor returned and nodded.

"The telegrams have been sent, Mr. Webster. There is really nothing you can do now. Unless you wish to detrain here and take the next train back to wherever you think your sister might be." He consulted his pocket watch. "The westbound train has already gone, but you can take the train tomorrow at 1:45 p.m."

Matthew pursed his lips. He had not thought of this possibility. But no, he had to reach Chicago for his business meetings.

He shook his head.

"No, I must go on to Chicago," he said.

He saw the conductor's look of surprise. Surely, the man did not think that he should change his travel plans to pursue a strange woman on a train, did he?

"Do you wish to contact the authorities in Troy and Kalispell regarding your sister's disappearance, Mr. Webster? If so, you must send a telegram now. The train leaves soon."

Matthew blinked. His sister... Yes, of course, the conductor would expect him to pursue the disappearance of his sister.

"Yes, I will do that, Conductor. Please do not let me keep you. I will see the station agent right away."

The conductor waved his watch as if to remind Matthew he was short on time before turning to leave the station.

Matthew regarded the station agent behind his counter, busily assisting arriving or departing passengers. Of course, he could not send a telegram to the authorities regarding a missing sister, as he had no sister. And he could hardly explain that Miss Reed had disappeared from his compartment as mysteriously as she had appeared.

Matthew waited a few moments and then reboarded the train. He returned to his compartment and tried to turn his attention to the business matters ahead in Chicago.

He was unable to concentrate though. Two images warred with each other for his attention, neither of which was a business associate. While Miss Reed had temporarily usurped Emily's position at the center of his thoughts, the pain of Emily's rejection continued its hold on his heart.

CHAPTER EIGHT

That afternoon, Walter had just gone outside to speak to one of the baggage handlers on the platform when Sara heard a strange sound behind her, like a series of clicks. She turned and noted a machine on a desk along the back wall. She got up to inspect it, noting brass fittings on a wood base. The sound came from a handle on one end. A telegraph! Apparently, Walter was getting a telegram. She wondered if she should go tell him.

Sara hurried out from behind the counter to find Walter. The main door of the station opened behind her, and she turned. A woman and a man entered the station.

Sara stilled. She hadn't dealt with any customers on her own, and she didn't think she could manage alone. She stuck her head out the door. Luckily, Walter stood nearby on the platform, talking to a big burley man.

"Walter," she whispered, beckoning him. "You have customers, and I think you have a telegram coming in."

Walter nodded, and with a final word to the baggage handler, he turned and entered the station.

"Mr. and Mrs. Feeney," he said warmly. "You've come to get your luggage."

Sara froze. Oh, please no!

Mrs. Feeney, a middle-aged, petite redhead, stared at her, her eyes focused on Sara's chest.

Walter caught the older woman's look.

"Mrs. Feeney, this is our new clerk, Miss Sara Reed," he said. "Miss Reed, Mr. and Mrs. Thomas Feeney. Mr. Feeney is a lawyer here in town."

"Oh!" Mr. Feeney, a tall, gawky and slender man, said as he held out his hand. "A lady clerk."

Sara accepted his handshake but watched Mrs. Feeney out of the corner of her eye. There had been other pieces of luggage in the storeroom. She had thought they'd been abandoned, had hoped they'd been abandoned. What had she been thinking?

"That blouse," Mrs. Feeney said. "I have one just like it. The lace is handmade."

Sara's eyes rounded, and she held her breath.

"Oh?" she breathed. Should she run now? Where to?

Out of the corner of her eye, she saw Walter tilt his head as he watched both women.

"Well, shall we get that case for you?" He turned to Sara. "The case was misplaced at the Chicago station a week ago, and we only just received it two days ago."

Sara said nothing but felt like she was going to pass out if she didn't take a breath soon.

Walter moved off to the storeroom. Sara would have at least escaped to the office if Mr. Feeney hadn't started asking her questions with a pleasant smile on his face.

"Are you new in town, Miss Reed?"

Sara nodded.

"Yes," she squeaked out. She kept an eye on the door, hoping against hope that Walter wasn't about to bring out the small brown case. But Walter produced the small brown case with a beam.

"I believe this is yours, Mrs. Feeney," he said.

"Yes, that's it, Mr. Wheeler. Thanks," Mr. Feeney said.

"Set it there, Mr. Wheeler. I want to look inside it," Mrs. Feeney said.

Sara, throwing a glance over her shoulder toward the front door, took a step backward.

"Don't you dare go anywhere!" Mrs. Feeney said sharply, staring at Sara.

Sara froze, as did Walter and Thomas. All three of them stared at Mrs. Feeney, but only Sara knew what was happening.

"My dear, what has come over you?" Mr. Feeney asked faintly.

"Mrs. Feeney, what—" Walter began, but he was cut off by a triumphant crow from Mrs. Feeney.

"That *is* my blouse," she said, lifting her attention from the bag and whirling around to face Sara. "*And* my skirt." She turned to Walter. "I don't know what sort of people you hire, Mr. Wheeler, but this woman has stolen clothing from my luggage!"

Walter turned to look at Sara. She wanted to cry. She wanted to run, but she could do neither.

"Is that true, Sara? Did you steal Mrs. Feeney's clothing from her case?"

Sara hung her head, lacing and interlacing her fingers. She gave a slight nod.

"Well, of course she did," Mrs. Feeney said. "Thomas, please go find the sheriff."

"Now, wait just a minute, my dear," Mr. Feeney reasoned. "Must we involve the sheriff? Surely if Miss Reed gives you back the clothing, that should suffice."

"I beg your pardon, Mrs. Feeney," Walter said with a heavy voice. "Miss Reed will be dismissed at once."

"See?" Mr. Feeney said. "She is dismissed, and I am certain she will be only too happy to return your clothing. I feel certain that is all that needs to be done."

"I want the sheriff!" Mrs. Feeney said stubbornly. "I don't want the clothing back, since it has come into contact with her person, but I want the sheriff!" She wrinkled her nose in distaste and anger.

Sara couldn't blame the woman. Her throat ached at the disappointment in Walter's face.

"I will go fetch him at once, my dear," Mr. Feeney said. He avoided looking at Sara.

"I can go change and give you the clothes," Sara began.

"Never!" Mrs. Feeney practically screeched.

"Mrs. Feeney, why don't you sit down while we wait for the sheriff?" Walter asked. "Is anything else missing from your luggage?"

Mrs. Feeney turned back to the case and snapped shut the locks before perching on the edge of the bench next to the case, her back as ramrod stiff as her resolve to see Sara arrested.

"No, everything else seems to be there, although in some disarray. I cannot believe the railroad hires thieves, Mr. Wheeler." She lifted her chin and turned away from both Walter and Sara.

"I am very sorry, Mrs. Feeney," Walter said with a sigh. "I understand your anger."

"I should hope so." She kept her face averted.

Sara looked up at Walter tentatively. What was going to happen to her?

"Sit down, Sara," he said, not unkindly. His face, already lined, seemed to have developed new creases.

Sara's mouth, already dry, screamed for water. She tried to lick her lips, but she just managed to rub dry skin on dry skin.

"I'll stand," she said thickly. She eyed the door, wondering if she could bolt.

"I would advise against it, Sara," Walter said quietly. Mrs. Feeney appeared not to hear.

Mr. Feeney reappeared in minutes.

"The sheriff is right behind me," he said. On cue, a large man, both in girth and height, strolled in. He sported a gray felt cowboy hat, dark-blue sturdy-looking trousers and a white cotton shirt under red suspenders. His dusty boots looked well worn. White hair and a broad white mustache on a weathered face completed his sheriff-of-a-Western-town look.

"Mrs. Feeney," he said with a nod. He eyed Sara with an assessing glance. "Walter. What's going on?"

Mrs. Feeney rose quickly. She stopped short of pointing at Sara with her index finger.

"Mr. Wheeler says she's an employee of the railroad. She stole some things from my luggage."

The sheriff turned to Walter.

"Is that true, Walter? Does she work for the railroad?"

"Miss Reed just started today, Bill. But I dismissed her as soon as I found out about the theft."

Rather than see the disappointment on Walter's face that his tone implied, Sara kept her eyes on her clasped hands.

"Do you have anything to say, young lady?"

Sara looked up. Steady blue eyes regarded her without expression. He seemed neither censuring nor sympathetic, but remarkably neutral.

"I'm sorry, Mrs. Feeney," she said. "I really am."

Mrs. Feeney turned a cold shoulder to her.

"You *are* going to arrest her, aren't you, Sheriff?"

"Most likely, Mrs. Feeney, unless you don't want to press charges?" The sheriff looked hopeful.

"Yes, I would most certainly like to press charges!" she blustered. Mr. Feeney looked down at the lobby floor as if he wished himself elsewhere.

Sara's stomach, already in a tight ball of anxiety, knotted still further.

"Well, that's that then. Come along, Miss Reed." He took Sara's arm, and she didn't resist. Who would resist such a big John Wayne kind of guy?

Sara avoided looking over her shoulder toward Walter. He didn't know her well, and he couldn't help her, even if he wanted. If anything, she had betrayed him, though she hadn't known him when she helped herself to Mrs. Feeney's clothes.

"The jail is just down here," the sheriff said as he kept a gentle but firm grip on her arm. He led the way down a wooden boardwalk toward what appeared to be the center of the town. False-fronted wooden buildings nestled between several two-storied red brick buildings. The structures at the town center flanked a dusty dirt road traversed by pedestrians, wagons and riders on horses. Kalispell seemed to be in the midst of expansion, as construction workers hammered away on the freshly cut timber of several new buildings.

Having seen some curious looks thrown their way and supposing that most people knew what it meant when the sheriff guided someone toward his office, Sara dropped her eyes and kept them on the boardwalk. She tripped over her skirts—Mrs. Feeney's skirts—several times until she learned to pull the skirts up with her free hand.

"What's your name?" the sheriff asked.

"Sara Reed," she said.

"I don't think I've seen you around town before, Miss Reed. Are you from Kalispell?"

Sara shook her head. "No. I'm from Spokane."

"So, what made you take the clothes? Seems like Walter had given you a pretty nice job there. You had to know you'd be the first person anyone would suspect if something went missing."

Sara chewed on her lip. What could she say?

"I needed the clothes. I didn't have any."

She kept her eyes down but felt the sheriff slow for a minute.

"You didn't have any? Well, you didn't walk into the station without clothing, did you?" His voice held a hint of humor.

Sara shook her head.

"No, but what I was wearing wasn't quite right."

"I don't know what that means, but I guess it doesn't matter. Mrs. Feeney is up in arms, and I have to arrest you."

"I understand," Sara said. She was actually growing resigned to the idea of being arrested. At least they would feed and house her. Or so she hoped. She couldn't think about the implications for the future. She couldn't even imagine what the next hour would hold.

They stopped in front of one of the false-fronted wooden buildings, and the sheriff guided her inside. A deputy of some sort jumped up and eyed them in surprise.

"Corbett," the sheriff said. "This is Miss Sara Reed. She is being arrested for theft."

Corbett, stocky and a little less tall than the sheriff, wore a fashionable black vest over a crisp white shirt. Dark-black trousers came to rest on the vamp of his shiny brown cowboy boots.

"Oh? What did she steal?" he asked over the top of Sara's head.

"Some stuff out of Mrs. Feeney's luggage down at the train station."
The sheriff propelled Sara through a wooden door and into a room
holding several cells. Thankfully, it was empty.

"Stuff? Like jewelry?" Corbett asked, following them.

"No, just some clothes," the sheriff said. He pulled open a door.

"Here you go, Miss Reed. Is there anyone I can contact for you? Any
family?"

Sara stepped into the cell as if in a dream. After all, her experience
couldn't possibly get any more bizarre.

Just like in the movies, the bed consisted of no more than a metal
frame holding a thin mattress covered by a dark dismal-colored woolen
blanket. No pillow or sheets were provided, and she supposed that was
actually a good thing. As Mrs. Feeney had wrinkled her nose when
looking at Sara, so Sara worried about bugs on the bedding.

The jail felt chilly, and she noted the walls were lined with brick
rather than the wood of the false front. She pulled her jacket more tightly
around her, finding the fleece insufficient against the cold. She supposed
she would have to wrap up in the blanket.

But for the moment, she pressed herself against the back wall as the
sheriff and Corbett waited for her response.

"No," she said. "No one."

"That can't be good," the sheriff said. "It's Friday. The judge went
down to Missoula for a week. I'm afraid you're stuck in here until then."

Sara nodded.

"Could I have some water?" she asked.

"Sure. Corbett, get her some water. Have you eaten?" the sheriff
asked. Corbett stepped out.

Sara nodded. "I ate lunch."

"Well, I'm about to go out for my lunch. I'll pick you up some hot
coffee to bring back." The sheriff turned back. "Do you have any other
clothes you want to wear? A bag? Something of your own anywhere?"

Sara shook her head. "No, nothing."

The sheriff rested his hands on the bars of the cell and leaned against
it.

"You don't *look* destitute, Miss Reed. You don't look like you've
been living in the wilderness. Where on earth did you come from?"

Sara shook her head. "The train? From Spokane."

He eyed her with a frown. "I'm guessing there's more to that story.
I'll be back in a while. Maybe you'll tell me about it when I get back."

Sara thought there was little chance of that.

Corbett delivered a metal cup of water, and Sara drank it gratefully.

"You sure don't look like a thief, Miss Reed."

Sara almost smiled.

"I'm not normally. Besides, what does a thief look like?" she asked, the words coming easier with every swallow of water.

He leaned against the doorframe and eyed her. Blond hair, cut short and parted in the middle, framed his boyish face. A starter mustache adorned his upper lip. She was sure he would grow into it someday.

"Well, not like *you*," he said.

Sara blinked. The young fellow was admiring her. She couldn't imagine what he saw in her to admire. She was half dressed, her hair was a mess, and she was an acknowledged thief. Were women in short supply in turn-of-the-century Kalispell, Montana?

CHAPTER NINE

"Next stop, Kalispell, Montana!" Matthew heard the conductor intone as he moved down the corridor past Matthew's compartment.

His business meetings in Chicago over the past two weeks had been productive, though they had failed to occupy his mind as thoroughly as he hoped. Thoughts of Emily—and the mysterious Miss Sara Reed—had weighed heavily on him.

He would have to come to terms with Emily's rejection of his marital proposal sooner rather than later. It would do no good to dwell. Though Emily did not wish to become his wife, he did not want to abandon their lifelong friendship, and he could not believe that Emily wanted that either.

As to Miss Reed, Matthew had not stopped thinking of her. By the time he detrained at Grand Central Station in Chicago, the conductor had failed to receive a response to his telegram from the Kalispell station. Matthew had made follow-up inquiries at the Grand Central, even insisting on sending another telegram, but if there had been a response, that seemed to go astray as well.

As a result, Matthew did not think well of the station agent in Kalispell, and he vowed to step off the train and speak to the agent in person, if only to give him a piece of his mind for the unprofessional lack of responses to his inquiries.

Had Miss Reed truly been his sister, Matthew would have been well within his rights to pursue her disappearance and to expect a timely response to his inquiries. If she had truly been his sister.

As the train slowed, Matthew rose and moved to the end of the car. He would have little time at the station to question the station agent, who would no doubt be busy with arriving and departing passengers. The conductor stood on the car platform watching the train's approach into the station. A different conductor than the one who had worked on the eastbound trip, the small bespectacled man tipped his cap with a pleasant smile.

"You're not getting off in Kalispell, are you, Mr. Webster? Seattle is your final destination, isn't it?"

"Yes, Conductor. I am bound for Seattle. I thought I might stretch my legs a bit in Kalispell," Matthew said. As the train came parallel with the station, the conductor leaned out and waved a hand toward the engineer. The train stopped with a cacophony of hissing steam and squealing wheels, and Matthew stepped down as soon as possible.

"Fifteen minutes, Mr. Webster," the conductor warned.

Matthew nodded and hurried into the station. As he feared, the agent behind the counter appeared to be busy with a line of passengers. Matthew knew he wouldn't have time to go to the back of the line.

"Pardon me," Matthew said as he stepped to the front counter. He nodded politely at the large portly gentleman now speaking to the agent.

"Pardon me, but this is an emergency. Please forgive me," he said to the gentleman. Matthew turned to the tall, white-haired agent who quirked a reproving eyebrow in Matthew's direction.

"Agent, several telegrams were sent to you regarding the disappearance of my sister, and to date there has been no response from you." By way of explaining his poor manners, Matthew spoke loudly enough for several people in line behind him to hear his words. Furthermore, he had not cared for the look of censure on the agent's face, an expression that now faded into one of shock.

Matthew's heart froze.

"Do you know her?" he asked hastily. "Miss Sara Reed? She disappeared from the train somewhere between Spokane and Havre. The Troy station said they had not seen her but could not swear that she did not detrain there."

The agent looked beyond Matthew to the now vocal group of passengers behind him.

"Sir, if you could just wait while I help these passengers, I could speak to you privately."

Matthew drew his brows together. "No!" He looked over his shoulder and addressed the waiting passengers. "Again, please forgive me, but I have very little time, and I must have an answer."

The gentleman behind him spoke.

"Yes, sir," he addressed Matthew. "We *all* have very little time if we want to catch the train, but *we* have waited in line. Agent, if you know something about this man's sister, kindly tell him and let us get on with our business."

The agent seemed to balk, but when he finally spoke, he leaned forward as if to speak only to Matthew.

"She is in jail, sir," he whispered.

"In jail?" Taken aback, Matthew barked out the question, instantly regretting his volume.

"Well, you have your answer, sir," the gentleman behind him said. "The jail is just up the street. You cannot miss it. Now, please kindly allow us to conclude our business so that *we* do not miss the train."

Matthew realized from the agent's sympathetic expression that he knew more but could not speak freely at the moment.

Matthew turned to look at the train, then toward the front door of the station. He checked his watch—11:10 a.m. He hurried back to the train, found his compartment and grabbed his overnight case. He managed to catch the attention of the porter.

"George, I am detraining here in Kalispell. Please see that my luggage is unloaded from the train and stored here at the station. I will pick it up shortly."

"Yes, sir," the porter said without expression. He hurried away, and Matthew stepped down from the train. Having made a spectacle of himself in the station and, worse yet, brought Miss Reed's name a measure of notoriety by forcing the agent to reveal her circumstances in public, he opted to circumnavigate the station to head for town.

He reached the main street and studied the signs on the buildings. Seeing the sign for the city jail, he moved in that direction, unsure of what he might find when he arrived, or what he meant to do. What had happened to the poor girl that necessitated her arrest? Surely stowing away aboard a train was not a crime worthy of incarceration, was it? Though she had disappeared, he had nevertheless paid for her fare to Chicago. Therefore, arrest was not warranted in that case.

He reached the wooden two-story building and paused at the doorway, marshalling his chaotic thoughts.

"Can I help you?" A young man dressed in the style of a cowboy pulled open the door of the jail.

"Oh!" exclaimed Matthew, momentarily taken aback. The young man must have seen him through the large plate glass window. "Yes, I was informed recently that my sister was incarcerated in your jail. I would like to see her."

The deputy, for his badge proclaimed him as such, lifted his sandy eyebrows in surprise.

"Miss Reed? Are you Sara's brother? I didn't know she had a brother. She never said anything."

Matthew frowned at the fellow's familiar use of Miss Reed's name.

"May I see her?" he asked again, his voice icy.

"Sure! Maybe you can do something to get her out of jail. I don't like the way she looks. She's been here quite a while."

Matthew's mouth went dry. Was she ill?

The deputy stood back and let him in. Matthew stepped inside the building, noting several wooden desks. A small fire blazed in a wooden stove, dispelling the chilly fall air.

"This way," the young man said. "I'm Deputy Corbett." He stepped through an open doorway to the rear of the office. On passing through the doorway, Matthew noted a sharp decrease in temperature.

"Sara!" Deputy Corbett called. "You have a visitor."

Matthew's heart rolled over as he viewed the cells. Miss Reed could not possibly have spent the last two weeks in this rather dank and dreary jail.

Deputy Corbett moved to the last cell.

"Sara, wake up! You have a visitor."

Matthew approached the cell and dropped his case at his feet. He grabbed the bars with a ferocity he did not know he possessed.

Miss Reed, lying huddled under a grayish blanket on a bed set against the back wall, lifted her head. Her brown hair, no longer shining, was pulled away from her face and rested on top of her head in haphazard fashion. Her face, once delicately colored, appeared pale and wan. Listless brown eyes stared at him for a moment.

"Miss—" Matthew caught himself. As her brother, he would not address her as Miss Reed.

"Sara," he called to her gently. "It is I, Matthew."

Miss Reed stared at him as if in confusion.

"Sara?" Deputy Corbett asked. "Is this your brother?"

"Of course I am her brother," Matthew snapped, terrified lest she denounce him. If he did not at least have the sanctity of family connections, he might not be able to help her.

"Sara, dearest, are you all right?" he asked softly.

Miss Reed pulled the blanket around her shoulders. She stood, revealing a wrinkled blouse underneath her coat and a skirt that hung loosely on her. She approached the bars, and Matthew let loose his grip and reached for her.

The blanket slipped from her shoulders as she took his hands. He closed firm fingers over her cold hands. Tears formed in her eyes and slipped down her face.

"Matthew," she whispered. "Oh, Matthew, I should never have left the train. I didn't mean to leave it."

Matthew, swallowing hard against his own unexpected anguish at her condition, gritted his teeth.

"Could you leave us for a moment, Deputy?" he said without taking his eyes from Miss Reed's face.

"I guess that will be okay," Corbett said. "I'll be right outside. We've been keeping the door open to try to warm the cells. There's no heat in here," he said.

"Thank you," Matthew said. The deputy stepped outside, and Matthew pulled Sara closer to the bars.

"My poor, dear Miss Reed," he murmured soothingly, his heart breaking as the tears flowed freely down her cheeks. "What terrible catastrophe occurred to bring you to this state?"

"I needed some clothes, and I stole some from Mrs. Feeney's luggage at the train station."

Matthew furrowed his brow as he quickly considered the implications of Miss Reed's words and predicament.

"Thank goodness!" he said, breathing a sigh of relief. "It is not as if you killed someone. This sort of thing can be dealt with."

Miss Reed shook her head.

"I don't think so, Matthew. She was pretty angry."

"Nonsense," he said with forced heartiness. She needed not his grief at her condition but his encouragement. "A few dollars here and there will make everything right, I am certain of it."

"I didn't have any money," Miss Reed said in a mournful tone.

"Have you been eating, Miss Reed? You have grown thin."

She shook her head. "I haven't had much of an appetite. My stomach has been tied in knots."

"My poor, dear Miss Reed," he murmured.

"How did you know I was here? Why are you here?"

"The station agent told me. I have searched for you since your disappearance from the train, but there was little I could do to find you from Chicago. I had hoped you were safe and in good health, but I see that neither is the case."

He enfolded both of her hands within his and rubbed them together to warm them.

"I must leave you now and rectify this situation. The sooner I have you out of here, the better."

He tried to pull his hands from hers, but she clung to him.

"I don't know why you're doing this for me," she said in a husky voice. "I can't pay you back, but I'll be forever grateful."

"You asked for my help two weeks ago, but I failed to help you," he said quietly.

She shook her head. "No, no, you did! That was me. I should never have left the train."

"Well, I can only hope that you will be able to tell me why you chose to leave the train rather than accept my assistance, but at the moment, I wish to speak to the authorities and Mrs. Feeney."

Miss Reed looked down. "I *am* a thief," she said.

"Made so by circumstance, I am certain," he said.

She released his hands and took a step back, crossing her arms over her stomach.

The whistle of the train caught both of their ears and gave Matthew the incentive to leave her.

"I will return as soon as possible," he said. He nodded reassuringly and left with reluctance. The deputy leaned on the edge of his desk, one booted foot crossed over the other.

"Has she had any medical treatment for her weight loss? For she surely has lost weight," Matthew said coldly.

"Sure, we've been taking pretty good care of her. She gets two meals a day from the café. The sheriff and me aren't happy about keeping her locked in here either, but the judge has been out of town for two weeks. He's due back tomorrow. The doctor says she's fine but that she hasn't been eating. He's right. She hardly touches the food."

Just then, a stalwart man also dressed Western-style stepped in and removed his cowboy hat to reveal a shock of white hair. His badge proclaimed him the sheriff.

"Howdy. Sheriff Langford," he said by way of introduction. "Can I help you?" He looked from Matthew to Deputy Corbett.

"He's here to see Sara," Corbett said. "Her brother."

Matthew extended a hand. He needed to gain this man's trust.

"Yes, Sara is my sister," he said pedantically. "Matthew Webster."

"Mr. Webster," the sheriff said with a raised brow.

"My half sister," Matthew offered automatically. "Can you tell me the details of her arrest?"

"Are you a lawyer, Mr. Webster?"

Matthew shook his head. "No, merely a businessman. But I wish to offer Mrs. Feeney compensation for what my sister stole in return for dropping the charges."

Sheriff Langford crossed his arms across his broad chest.

"You're welcome to try, of course, but Mrs. Feeney is pretty angry. I doubt she would accept any sort of money. As far as what happened, it seems that your sister got into the luggage storeroom at the station and stole clothes out of Mrs. Feeney's luggage. Mrs. Feeney saw Miss Reed in the clothing and recognized it as hers."

"The luggage storeroom? Why would she go in there?"

"Well, she *was* working there—had just started the day she was arrested, in fact."

"Working at the station?" Matthew shook his head as if to clear it. "Doing what?"

"As a clerk. Walter had just hired her that morning. Said she was wearing the clothing when he hired her. He had no idea when she got into the storage room. She really hasn't said much about it, just that she needed the clothing."

From the sheriff's frank appraisal of Matthew's attire, he could tell the sheriff was wondering how his sister found herself in such dire straits that she must steal clothing.

Matthew could not offer any explanation that might seem remotely reasonable, not to the sheriff, not even to himself, and he did not try.

"So, it is agreed that if I am successful in convincing Mrs. Feeney to drop the charges against my sister, you will release her."

The sheriff shrugged. "I'd be happy to," he said. "I don't really think she belongs here, and I've been hoping someone would come to her aid. How did you find out she was in jail? She didn't send for you though, did she? I would have known about it."

Matthew shook his head. "No, she did not. She disappeared from the train two weeks ago. We...we were on a journey to Chicago, and she vanished from the train somewhere in Montana...in Kalispell I now know. We telegraphed the station agent here but received no response."

"Vanished?" the sheriff said. "How?"

Matthew shrugged. "I cannot say. I have not had much chance to talk to her. I thought she might have been kidnapped, but it appears not."

Sheriff Langford gave him a skeptical look.

"You mean she walked off the train voluntarily and didn't tell you she was getting off?"

Matthew swallowed hard. He could think of only one response to offer, and Miss Reed would certainly not like it.

"My sister has been troubled of late," he said. "A thwarted romance, a broken heart. I cannot say more." That he had vested Miss Reed's situation with a description of his own broken heart would not sit well with her, but perhaps she might never hear of it.

The sheriff nodded. "That is a shame," he said. "Yes, I understand now."

"No wonder she hasn't been eating," Corbett offered, his young face a vision of sympathy. "A broken heart will put you off your feed every time, that's for sure."

Matthew regarded the young deputy with something less than

warmth. He had been far too familiar with Miss Reed, and Matthew could not approve.

"Yes," he said shortly. "Sheriff, if you could give me Mrs. Feeney's direction, I hope to resolve this matter today and remove my sister to a hotel."

"Maybe you should talk to Mrs. Feeney's husband first. He's an attorney. He could probably help you reason with her. He really didn't want to see Miss Reed in jail any more than the rest of us did."

"Yes, that will do nicely," Matthew said.

Moments later, armed with Mr. Feeney's address, Matthew left the jail, his thoughts occupied with several ideas for reparations which might interest Mrs. Feeney, ranging anywhere from mere monetary compensation to a free round-trip shopping expedition to Seattle, even more if necessary. Anything to secure Miss Reed's freedom from jail.

CHAPTER TEN

"I don't even want to know how you got her to drop the charges," Sara said two hours later as she left the jail with Matthew. "I'm just so grateful that you did." She paused on the boardwalk just outside of the jail with the awful feeling that everyone stared at her, knowing she was a thief.

"No, wait," she said. "How *did* you get me out, Matthew?"

Matthew adjusted his hat and looked down at her with an enigmatic expression.

"It was no trouble, truly. I had a short conversation with Mr. Feeney, who consulted with his wife. I offered them a modest compensation for the clothing and Mrs. Feeney's ruffled feathers, and the deed was done."

Matthew smiled briefly as he spoke, but Sara thought his blue eyes glittered just a bit. She couldn't believe that Mrs. Feeney had accepted just a "modest compensation."

"How modest?"

Matthew put an arm under her elbow.

"Come, Miss Reed, let us find a hotel for you. We cannot linger in front of the jail."

Sara allowed him to lead her down the boardwalk toward a two-storied brick building nestled between several other buildings. Green awning-covered windows faced the main street, and a matching green awning over the front door sported the regal title Hotel Excelsior.

Sara balked at entering the hotel. Matthew's comfort with wealth in the early twentieth century threatened to sweep her away into a world she did not understand. She needed to slow him down a bit.

"Wait!" she said. "Wait. I need a minute."

Matthew dropped his hand from her elbow and turned to face her. He set his small overnight case down, the one she had seen on the overhead rack in his train compartment.

"What troubles you, Miss Reed?"

Sara dropped her eyes to the toes of her canvas shoes peeping out from beneath her skirt.

"I don't know. I just feel...rushed," she said. "I have to think."

Matthew clasped his hands behind his back, and Sara looked up at him with a wince and a shrug.

"I know I seem ungrateful, and I'm not," she said. "I'm truly grateful for everything you're doing for me, but I need a minute to think about things."

"What 'things' confuse you, Miss Reed?"

"Everything at the moment," she said ruefully. She watched as well-dressed guests walked in and out of the hotel, their elevated economic status reflected in the touches of satin, velvet and lace on their clothing.

"I don't know why you're doing all this for me," she murmured. "I can't just take your charity."

Matthew cocked his head and grimaced.

"You asked for my help," he said simply.

Sara grimaced. "I did, I know, but I had no idea I would become such a burden. I was desperate at the time."

"And yet you disappeared," he said.

Matthew hadn't yet asked her about the clothing or why she had left the train, but she suspected he would. She had nothing to offer him. No excuses, no stories. She hadn't had time to concoct some plausible tale, nor did she really have the energy. She was physically and emotionally exhausted from her weeks in the jail—from inactivity, cold and lack of appetite as well as hoping, wishing and praying that she could get out of the mess she was in by traveling back to the future.

"I did," she said with a faint nod. She avoided his eyes but knew he watched her.

"You need rest, Miss Reed. You need a hot bath, food, warmth and sleep, in that order."

His words sounded wonderful, but still she hesitated.

"And then what?" She looked up at him then. Why was he helping her? If this had been the twenty-first century, and a handsome man offered her a stay in a hotel, she would have immediately suspected an ulterior motive.

As if he could read her mind, Matthew turned to look toward the hotel and then drew in a sharp breath. "I trust you do not think you are indebted to me in any way, Miss Reed. I simply want to ensure your safety and comfort. I do not know what has befallen you to bring you to this state, and perhaps some day you will tell me, but until then, I only want to help."

"I wish I could tell you, Matthew, but I can't. And I don't know how I can pay you back," she murmured.

"Do not worry about that now, Miss Reed. Come," he said with a gentle hand at the back of her waist urging her forward.

"It's a small town," Sara said. "Do you think everyone knows?"

"Knows about..."

"Me," she said. "The clothes, Mrs. Feeney."

"I trust not," he said, "but I cannot guarantee that Mrs. Feeney has not shared her...misfortunes about the town."

Sara sighed heavily. "I really should apologize to her," she mumbled.

"There really is no need," Matthew said. "The less you see of that woman, the better."

Sara looked up at Matthew to see his jaw set into a firm line.

"Oh! It was a tough sell, I guess."

"It is over. Shall we?" Again, he urged her forward, and Sara allowed him to propel her through the door.

They stepped inside, and Sara drew in a sharp breath. The modest exterior didn't do justice to the fairly opulent interior. Ruby-red carpets covered most of the highly varnished wooden lobby floor. A long counter in a dark wood like mahogany flanked one wall. Comfortable-looking easy chairs grouped around small coffee tables filled the rest of the large lobby.

The hotel bustled with activity as guests checked in or out, porters carried luggage, and other guests took tea, coffee or drinks in the lounge area of the lobby.

Sara felt extremely self-conscious in her wrinkled, ill-fitting clothing, and she was sure she caught several glances thrown her way from women. That she hadn't had a shower in two weeks only worsened matters. She knew her hair was matted, and she hoped she didn't smell as bad as she felt. The soap and pail of cold water Corbett had brought her on a daily basis had served only as a sponge bath, and a poor one at that, as she had worried someone would come into the cell while she was washing.

Matthew guided her purposefully through the throng and up to the desk.

"Good afternoon. I would like two rooms for my sister and myself," he said to the middle-aged desk clerk. A small man with glasses, the clerk's eyes narrowed, and his welcoming smile faded when he looked at Sara.

Sara swallowed hard, ran a hand down the frilly front of her wrinkled blouse and tried to tuck herself out of sight behind Matthew.

"Yes, sir." The clerk tore his eyes from Sara to return them to Matthew's face.

"Names, please?"

"Mr. Matthew Webster and Miss Sara Reed."

The clerk, who had bent to consult a ledger, looked up quickly and stared hard at Sara. His nose twitched, and he shook his head.

"I am sorry, sir, but we do not have any available rooms."

"I beg your pardon?" Matthew said as if he hadn't heard the clerk right. "No rooms at all?"

"No, sir," the clerk said, his eyes sliding toward Sara again.

Sara tugged at Matthew's sleeve.

"Let's go. It's because of me," she whispered.

"Nonsense," Matthew said, drawing himself even taller than he already was. "I wish to speak to the owner of this hotel."

The clerk pursed his lips. "Yes, of course. Just a moment, please." He straightened his tie and tugged at his jacket as he turned to head for a door behind the counter.

Sara, wishing the floor would swallow her up, peeked out from behind Matthew. Luckily, no one waited behind them.

A tall, slender, gray-haired woman, dressed all in black, emerged from the doorway, followed by the clerk.

"Yes, sir, I'm Mrs. Calloway. How can I help you?" Her eyes flitted over Sara before settling on Matthew. The desk clerk hovered at her elbow.

"My sister and I would like to have two rooms. Your clerk stated you have no rooms available," Matthew said briefly. "I wonder if you could check again."

Mrs. Calloway didn't even bother to consult the ledger. She directed a sidelong glance at Sara before responding.

"No, I am sorry. We do not have any rooms available."

Without touching him, Sara could feel the tension in Matthew's body.

"Very good," Matthew said. "Is there another hotel nearby?"

Mrs. Calloway pursed her lips, much as the desk clerk had done.

"There are others in Kalispell," she said unhelpfully. "But I am not sure they will take a thief."

They knew! Everyone knew! Sara swung around and ran out the front door, turning to the right without any idea where she was headed. A strong hand grabbed her arm, stilling her. She knew it was Matthew.

She turned blindly, tears streaming down her face, and Matthew pulled her into his arms.

"Forgive me for taking you to such an abysmal hotel, Miss Reed. I am so sorry to subject you to such ill-mannered boorishness."

Sara buried her face against the smooth surface of his overcoat.

"Everybody knows!" she muttered against his chest. "Everybody knows!"

"Surely not everybody," Matthew murmured. She heard the rumble of his voice in his chest. "Small towns, etcetera."

He released her and produced a handkerchief from a pocket in his suit jacket.

Sara, wishing he'd come up with a tissue so she could blow her nose, took the handkerchief, dabbed at her eyes and handed it back with a sniff.

"Well, let us explore then," Matthew said. "Surely, there must be some establishment that Mrs. Feeney has not yet influenced with her gossip, because I am sure that is what happened. Had I known that when she withdrew her complaint, I would have pursued some sort of nondisclosure measure."

"Well, I'm sure everyone knew about it long before you arrived."

"Yes, more is the pity," he said. "There is another hotel." He propelled her forward toward another brick building further down the street, but he acquiesced when she insisted on staying outside.

He returned within minutes.

"We have rooms!" he said, dangling two sets of keys. "The hotel is not what I am used to, but it will do. I gave your name as Sara Webster. I hope you do not mind. I apologize for this subterfuge, but I do not wish to see you humiliated again."

"I still have to get through the lobby," Sara said with a rueful smile. "I doubt my picture is plastered on the post office wall, but I do look pretty awful."

"Stealing clothing is hardly a hanging offense," Matthew said with a matching wry smile. "And I am certain your photograph is not affixed to a wanted poster."

The corner of Sara's mouth twitched for the first time since she'd found herself in the depths of a time-traveling nightmare.

"So, how are we going to sneak me in?" she asked. She dropped her eyes as several men exited the hotel.

"Boldly, on my arm," Matthew said. His deep-throated chuckle, the first she'd ever heard from him, warmed her heart like no hot bowl of soup ever could. Things suddenly looked much brighter, though nothing had really changed. Matthew held out his arm, and Sara tucked her hand underneath.

She ran her free hand along the surface of her hair to smooth it as she and Matthew stepped into the hotel. Not as grand as the first hotel, the lobby of the Kalispell Arms appeared to cater to travelers who did not have the luxury of lace, velvet and satin trim on their clothing.

As with the Excelsior, several guests relaxed in the lobby, sipping tea, coffee and drinks. The carpets were a subdued cobalt blue, and the furnishings a bit more utilitarian than that of the Excelsior.

Matthew strolled boldly past the desk clerk, a stout man whose back was turned to the lobby as he sorted through room key slots on the wall behind the counter.

They reached the stairs without a shout of "thief" and ascended to the second floor. Matthew stopped in front of one room and inserted the key. He pushed open the door and stepped in.

"I hope this will do," he said, awaiting Sara's approval.

"I'm a beggar," Sara said with a twitch of her lips. "Anything but a jail cell will do." She stepped into the room. A brass double bed with a pale-blue quilt dominated the small room. A well-polished dresser flanked one side of the room, and a small desk and straight-back chair rested against the other wall.

"I believe these rooms have their own bathrooms," Matthew said. He opened a door and looked in. "Yes."

Sara peeked in. The bathroom, though small by twenty-first-century standards, was not markedly different from others that she had used. The claw-foot tub looked inviting.

"They do have hot and cold running water, unlike some of the smaller hotels," Matthew said.

Sara thought about that statement. In her time, few people asked if a hotel had hot and cold running water...at least not in Spokane.

"Is that unusual?" she asked as she turned back to survey the room. Festive blue drapes in a flower pattern hung from the single window that looked out over the main street.

"Hot and cold running water?" Matthew asked. "You cannot have traveled much, Miss Reed, if you have not had to ask the hotel staff to have hot water delivered for your bath." A charming smile of even, white teeth lightened his face, and Sara drew in a steadying breath as she looked at him. He didn't wear a mustache as so many of his contemporaries did, and he was that much handsomer for it.

The irony of his statement was not lost on her.

"No," she said. "I guess I haven't traveled much."

Matthew handed her the key to the room. "I am just next door," he said. "I asked the clerk to have some food, tea and coffee sent up in about an hour. Will that be sufficient time for you to attend to your needs?"

By needs, Sara assumed he meant a bath. She looked down at her clothes, the blouse and skirt that had gotten her into so much trouble. She couldn't bear to put them back on, not only because they stank from the dingy mattress at the jail, but because they were a constant reminder of her shame...her theft.

She looked up at Matthew helplessly, hoping he would understand her wordless plea. He did.

"Yes, I have been giving that some thought," he said, chewing on his lower lip as he studied her wrinkled skirt. "Emily would know what to do," he said, almost as if to himself.

"Emily?" Sara asked.

Matthew blinked and looked up.

"I beg your pardon?"

"You said 'Emily would know what to do.'"

His cheeks took on a bronze tinge.

"Did I? How silly of me. I cannot think why. I do not have sisters and have no experience with shopping for women's clothing. Emily is an old friend, and perhaps I spoke my thoughts aloud. I think I must find a shop in town that sells ready-to-wear women's clothing. There is such a thing, is there not?"

Sara's eyes widened.

"I have no idea," she said. "Well, I don't know about Kalispell," she amended hastily.

"But are there such shops in Spokane? I know there are gentlemen's stores in Seattle where one can purchase ready-to-wear shirts in the appropriate size. Suits and trousers must still be tailored, of course."

"Oh, there must be," Sara mumbled. She had no earthly idea what was available at the turn of the century. None. Not hot and cold running water, not ready-to-wear clothing, not a way to get back home.

CHAPTER ELEVEN

Matthew left Miss Reed to attend to her needs, and he returned to the lobby to speak to the desk clerk who had introduced himself as Gerry Martin.

"Yes, I wonder if you know of any women's clothing stores that sell ready-to-wear clothing? My sister is in need of a few new dresses, and I wish to surprise her for her birthday."

Matthew smiled pleasantly, hoping Gerry could not see the deceit on his face.

"Yes, sir, there's a few. The Emporium is just across the street. My wife shops there, comes home with ready-made dresses all the time. Running me into the poorhouse with her shopping, she is."

Matthew, on the point of hurrying from the hotel, turned back with a broad smile to regard Gerry. At about sixty years of age, the clerk's thick gray mustache and beard framed a face as round as his belly. He smiled readily and had done so when Matthew checked in.

"My sympathies," Matthew said.

Gerry held up a beefy hand. "I'm joking. She enjoys shopping, and I don't deny her anything. She's the love of my life," he said. Already ruddy cheeks brightened even more, and his blue eyes twinkled.

Matthew swallowed hard and repressed a sigh. He had thought Emily was the love of his life. Would that he could send her shopping and admire the clothing she modeled for him at the end of the day.

"You are a fortunate man," Matthew said.

"Don't I know it!" Gerry responded with a self-satisfied nod. "I was a lonely timber man pining for some long-lost love back East. Then Dorothy got off the train here one day. I met her, fell in love, and I never looked back."

Matthew envied the contented smile on the clerk's face.

"And you lived happily ever after," Matthew murmured, momentarily forgetting his task.

"You could say that."

A couple approached the counter, and Matthew snapped out of his reverie of imagining Emily and himself in such a contented and blissful marriage. He nodded to both Gerry and the new arrivals, and he hurried out the door.

As Gerry had said, The Emporium was just across the street. He rushed to the shop and stepped in.

"Good day, sir. Can I help you?" a petite, birdlike woman asked as she hurried to greet him. The shop was narrow but deep, as the wooden building was sandwiched between two larger red brick buildings. Long wooden counters and shelves along the walls held stacks of colorful cloth. A mannequin stood by the front window, attired in a lovely peach silk gown.

"Yes, thank you," Matthew said, his mouth suddenly dry. How on earth did one order women's clothing? "My sister is in need of a few new things. I wish to surprise her. I need them right away."

"What sort of things does she need?" the clerk asked.

Matthew gestured toward the shop in general. "Whatever it is that women wear," he said in a deliberately airy manner. "Some dresses, a coat of some sort, undergarments." His face heated at the last words.

"Oh!" the woman responded, a bright smile lighting her face. "I'm Mrs. Knowles. And you are?"

"Matthew Webster," he said with a brief incline of his head. "It is a pleasure to meet you, Mrs. Knowles. I hope you can help me."

"Yes, indeed we can. Can your sister come into the shop? I would need to take her measurements. We have some fine patterns and lengths of material that I think would make exquisite dresses, all in the latest styles."

Matthew put up a restraining hand. "No, I need something today," he said.

"Today?" Mrs. Knowles squeaked. "Oh!"

"Yes, in fact, I need something immediately," Matthew said. "I was told you might have some ready-to-wear clothing?"

Mrs. Knowles, looking crestfallen at the demise of her grand plan to create clothing in the "latest styles," nodded. "Well, yes, we do have a few things, but we would need to adjust the hem of the skirts to fit your sister's height."

Matthew shook his head. "Perhaps tomorrow or another day. For now, I need something immediately."

"Good gracious, Mr. Webster. Surely, your sister is not without something to wear as we speak!"

Matthew, his patience growing thin, took a deep breath.

"Mrs. Knowles, I know I can rely upon your discretion. It is my sister's birthday today. I forgot to get her a present, and I do not want her to know. I have to bring something. I was so hoping you might have a few things I could give her today."

The clerk nodded sagely. "Yes, of course. Although I think a pretty shawl would be more than enough, I understand your dilemma. Let me see show you a few dresses. If they need tailoring, you may bring your sister to see me."

"Thank you!" Matthew said. "And a pretty shawl would be nice, as well as a coat. And the other things I mentioned."

"You are a generous brother, Mr. Webster," the clerk said as she led him toward a counter.

Forty-five minutes later, Matthew left the store under the weight of six boxes as Mrs. Knowles held the door open and waved him off with a happy face. He returned to the hotel and staggered past Gerry, who came out from behind the counter to help.

"I see Mrs. Knowles got her hooks into you," the clerk laughed. "I should have warned you about her."

Matthew allowed Gerry to take a few boxes. "Yes, she's quite the saleswoman," he said, "but very helpful."

"Let me help you carry these upstairs," Gerry said with a glance over his shoulder. "We don't have a porter here at the hotel, but I can step away from the desk for a minute. I did send a boy to the train station to pick up your case, as you requested on checking in, and it's waiting for you in your room. Are you certain your sister didn't have a case?"

Matthew shook his head, already forming another lie.

"No, her luggage was lost on the train."

Gerry clucked and shook his head. "That's not particularly unusual," he said. "You notified the station agent, Walter, right?"

Matthew cursed silently. Lost luggage was perhaps not the best excuse he could have given. The station agent was fully aware of Miss Reed's present predicament with luggage.

"Yes," he responded shortly. They climbed the stairs.

"Your food should be ready soon," Gerry said.

Matthew looked at him blankly.

"The food you ordered for yourself and your sister? To be delivered to your room?"

Matthew shook his head as if to rid himself of cobwebs. Normally an organized man, he was making a shambles of the day.

"Oh, that is right. Thank you so much. I had better hurry upstairs then." He hoped to have time for a bath and shave before the food arrived. What would Miss Reed think of him, presenting himself disheveled as he was?

They stopped outside of Miss Reed's door.

"Thank you, Gerry," Matthew said as he took the boxes from him. "I think I can manage now."

Gerry nodded. "Let me know if you need anything else, Mr. Webster."

"Thank you."

Matthew waited until the clerk had disappeared down the hall and out of sight before tapping on Miss Reed's door.

"Who is it?" a small voice asked.

"Matthew," he said. "I am alone. I come bearing gifts." Despite the chaos of the day, he smiled whimsically, deriving a certain pleasure as though he were truly presenting a beloved sister with a birthday present.

The door opened a crack, and Miss Reed, wet curls hanging to her shoulders, peeped out before opening the door wide. She had bathed but donned the soiled clothing once again.

Matthew stepped in and dropped the boxes onto the bed.

"There! I do hope the clothing fits. If not, Mrs. Knowles at The Emporium across the street will tailor them for you. I had to guess at the appropriate sizes."

Miss Reed smiled brightly. "Thank you so much!" she said. She moved to open the first box. "You have no idea what this means to me. Mrs. Feeney's clothing is like a scarlet letter."

Matthew understood her reference.

"I can only imagine." He watched as she pulled the peach silk gown from the box and held it up. Her freshly scrubbed cheeks took on the same hue as the gown.

"Oh, my word," she breathed as she looked from the gown to him.

"It was ready-to-wear," Matthew said in a husky voice. He cleared his throat. "There are a few day dresses in that lot as well."

He turned. "I must go bathe before our late luncheon arrives. I was not certain I could obtain clothing, and I thought you might be more comfortable eating in your room rather than facing a crowd in the dining room," he said. "I do hope you enjoy the clothing."

"Thank you, Matthew," Miss Reed said again as she laid the dress carefully down on the bed. "Thank you for everything. I don't know how I'll ever pay you back."

"Nonsense," he said gruffly. "I will return shortly."

He closed the door behind him and moved down the hall to his own room, a replica of Miss Reed's room. He shed his clothing, bathed quickly and rummaged in his case for a fresh shirt and a dark-brown suit, thinking himself fortunate that he had the good sense to have his clothes laundered in Chicago before he left.

Dressed as quickly as he had ever done, he presented himself to Miss Reed's room in twenty minutes. A tray had been set outside her door, and he picked it up and tapped on the door, feeling much like a waiter.

"Who is it?" she called out.

"Matthew," he said.

"Ummm," she murmured, closer now to the door. "I'm not quite dressed."

"Oh!" he said. He looked down at the tray in his hand, feeling quite foolish. Perhaps he should not have ordered the food until they were both bathed and dressed. The pandemonium of the day had truly forced him into poor decisions.

"Someone knocked on the door earlier. Said he was leaving a tray of food?"

"Yes, I have it here," Matthew said, uncertain of what to do.

"Oh, really? It's probably getting cold then. You can bring it in, but be forewarned—I'm not completely dressed."

Matthew threw a harried look down the hall but no one was about. He leaned closer to the door and whispered.

"Miss Reed, I cannot enter your room if you are not dressed. Shall I take the tray to my room and await your convenience?"

"Well, you could, but I'm not sure I'd be dressed anytime tonight if I don't get your help. I've tried and tried, but I can't get the blouse buttoned in the back."

Matthew drew in a sharp breath and scanned the hall quickly.

"Yes, all right, let me in, Miss Reed," he said hastily.

She opened the door, a vision in a lovely ivory shirtwaist blouse, trimmed in antique lace, and a rose taffeta skirt. Around her shoulders she had draped the shawl Mrs. Knowles had selected for him, a beautiful paisley confection in shades of blue and rose. Her hair, still damp, continued to drape over her shoulders in an unruly fashion.

He set the tray down on the dresser and turned to her.

Miss Reed's cheeks, as rosy as her skirt, glowed, and he drew in a steadying breath.

"How may I assist you?" he asked.

She pointed to the back of her neck.

"The blouse—I can't get it buttoned."

Matthew stepped around behind her. With unsteady hands, he slipped the paisley shawl from her shoulders, pushed her hair aside and fastened the remaining buttons at the back of her blouse. She had managed to fasten the buttons at the neck and waist of the blouse, so he had little left to do. To his regret.

"There," he said in a throaty voice.

"Thank you," Miss Reed murmured as she dropped the shawl to the bed. "And thank you again for the clothing. There were some pieces I didn't know what to do..." She pressed her lips together and shook her head as if responding to an internal dialogue.

"Pieces?" he queried.

"What?" she asked, suddenly moving across the room to examine the tray of food. "I'm starving. Coffee?" she asked, picking up a small porcelain pot.

"Yes, please," Matthew said, certain that she prevaricated but unsure about what. "Do the skirts need hemming?"

Miss Reed looked down at her garment, clearly bemused.

"No, they fit fine. I can walk in them."

She poured him a cup of coffee, and they each took a plate.

"I did not think the rooms would be so small," Matthew said as he searched for a suitable seating area.

"We can eat at the desk," Miss Reed said. "There's an extra chair against the wall there. How's your room? Is it the same?"

Matthew waited until she sat and then seated himself.

"Yes, identical to yours."

Miss Reed bit into her food.

"I am pleased to see that you have an appetite," Matthew said. "I was not sure what I would do if you continued to fast."

"I couldn't eat in there," she said with a grimace. "My stomach was in knots, not knowing what was going to happen to me. Again, I can't thank you enough for what you've done for me, Matthew. If there is anything I can do to pay you back, I'll do it."

Matthew shook his head. Ironically, he now found his own appetite diminished as he surreptitiously watched her eat while making a pretense at his own food. She pushed back her hair when it fell in her face. Nut brown, with soft tendrils that framed her face, he now knew it to be as silky as it looked.

"I am afraid I did not acquire any sort of pins and such for your hair," he said. "Will you require some? Miss Knowles did send one hat to match the coat she selected. A charming confection of brown and blue."

"Pins?" she asked. She put a hand to her hair. "Oh, that's right. I have to put it up, don't I?"

Matthew cocked his head. "I believe so," he said. "I know Emily had to put her hair up when she was about eighteen years old. She hated that day, having enjoyed a fairly hoydenish childhood. I hated it as well, but only because I could no longer pull her blonde hair as I did when we were younger."

Lost in reminiscing, Matthew looked up to see Miss Reed staring at him.

"Forgive me," he said hastily. "My thoughts wandered."

"Tell me about Emily," Miss Reed said.

Matthew pressed his lips together, his appetite well and truly gone now.

"There is not much to tell," he said with a heavy sigh. He stared at the food on his plate. "Emily lives next door. An only child, as am I, we spent many hours together as children playing. We were inseparable. At some point during our teenage years, I came to believe that Emily and I would marry, though I never gave it much thought. I believe our families expected the same thing. I never said anything. It just seemed to be the natural progression of our lives, our future."

He sighed heavily again.

"Two weeks ago on the eve of my trip to Chicago, I proposed to Emily. She rejected me, stating that while she loved me like a brother, she could not envision me as a husband. The next day, I boarded the train. I have not seen or heard from her since."

In the silence that ensued, Matthew looked up to find Miss Reed watching him with a sympathetic face. He cleared his throat.

"I'm so sorry," she said. "Is there any chance she'll change her mind?"

"I am afraid not," Matthew said. "If nothing else, Emily has always known her own mind. I have never imagined a future in which she did not play a part. I feel bereft somehow." He laughed without mirth. "One would think I had lost my best friend."

"Well, it sounds like you did," Miss Reed said.

CHAPTER TWELVE

Sara lost her appetite and wiped at her mouth with the linen napkin.

So, Matthew was in love...and from the sounds of it, heartbroken as well. She supposed it was too much to hope that such a handsome man had been waiting around for *her* to show up. She looked at him from under veiled lashes.

His chestnut brown hair, freshly washed and now drying, gleamed. Parted on the side and immaculate as always, Sara wondered what he looked like upon awakening in the morning with tousled hair. Long dark sideburns, the color of his thick eyebrows, tapered to just below his ears and gave his face an angular but elegant look. His aquamarine eyes watched her now, and she turned away to look toward the window so he wouldn't see her disappointment.

"Yes, I suppose you are correct, Miss Reed. Emily has always been there, first as my childhood playmate, then the woman I planned to marry."

Sara drew in a deep breath and let it out slowly. It shouldn't have mattered to her if some stranger was in love with another woman, especially a stranger from the past. She hardly knew Matthew. But something bothered her, something other than the fact that she was lost in time. She recognized the feeling as jealousy.

"I'm sorry," Sara murmured, unable to come up with anything particularly profound.

"Thank you," Matthew said quietly. "It is a relief to speak of it to someone. I have not told anyone since I left Seattle. My parents will be most disappointed to hear we are not to marry, if they have not heard from Emily already, though I doubt she would mention my proposal to them. She knew their hopes for us."

"Are you close to your parents?" Sara asked, a lump forming in her throat. She missed her mother and had never known her father, a youthful infatuation of her mother's who had long since disappeared.

"Yes, I am," Matthew said. "I am an only child. My mother could not have more children, and she doted on me." His smile was gentle as he spoke of his mother.

"And you?" he asked. "Are you close to your mother? You stated she is 'single.' Is she widowed?"

A tear slipped down Sara's face, and she wiped it away and blinked back the rest.

"Yes," she murmured. "I was very close to my mother. She passed away a year ago. She'd been sick for a long time."

"Oh, my dear Miss Reed, I am so very sorry."

Sara gritted her teeth and smiled tremulously.

"She wasn't a widow, no. My parents weren't married. I never knew my father."

Matthew drew in a sharp breath before falling silent.

Sara dragged her eyes back from the window and looked at him. His lips were pressed together as if he didn't know what to say.

"Are you shocked?" she said, her grief evolving into anger. "Don't be. That's *my* business, not yours. My father abandoned her when he found out she was pregnant, but she didn't abandon me. I'm proud of her and always will be. She's the greatest role model I could ever have!"

Sara had given the same speech on more than one occasion in her life, in elementary school and in high school, to girls whose parents were unhappily married or divorced. She shouldn't have been surprised to find shock on the face of a turn-of-the-century man.

Matthew's cheeks bronzed, and he ran a hand across his face.

"My expression betrayed me, I see," he said ruefully. "Forgive me, Miss Reed. Truly. I do not mean to sit in judgment upon your beloved mother. I was merely surprised, that is all."

Having channeled some of the demons from her childhood, Sara calmed down instantly at the sincerity on Matthew's face.

"I'm sorry," she said. "I'm defensive about my mom, about my parentage. I took a lot of flack in school about being 'illegitimate,' as they say. It's hardly an issue anymore though. No one cares."

She looked up from a contemplation of her knuckles to see Matthew chewing on his lower lip. What a stupid statement! Of course, people still cared...in nineteen hundred.

"Well, not so much in Spokane anyway," she amended.

"At the risk of incurring your displeasure, I must say that I did not realize Spokane was such a broad-minded city," Matthew said with a twitch at the corner of his lips.

"Oh, yes," she said airily. Of course, it wasn't. Spokane, a city on the east side of Washington state, formerly centered around farming and ranching, was known to be fairly conservative, unlike the more liberal Seattle on the West Coast. She hoped Matthew would drop the subject.

"I see," he said, but he didn't look as if he agreed. "Tell me about your family in North Dakota. These are relatives of your mother?"

Sara laced and unlaced her fingers under the table. "Yes," she said with a nod. "My mother's aunt and some cousins."

"Are you close to them? Do you see them often?"

"Yes," she said without thinking.

"I wonder why you got off the train but did not continue on to North Dakota."

Sara, her mouth suddenly dry, drank some water while she thought of a response. She was running out of imagination.

"Well, I...I..." She took another drink. Matthew watched her carefully. Unable to come up with anything, she jumped up and crossed the room to look down at the street below. For a small city, traffic bustled in the form of wagons, horses and pedestrians.

"Do you mind if I don't talk about it?" she finally turned and asked.

Matthew rose and came to stand beside her.

"But of course, Miss Reed. I should not insist. I am only concerned for your future welfare. I cannot stay in Kalispell for long, and I am loathe to leave you here without protection, without income and without family."

Sara wanted to say she would be fine, but she didn't think she would. She knew she couldn't get a job anywhere else, not with a reputation as a thief. At some point, Matthew would have to return to his home, his job, but she hadn't thought that far ahead.

"I have to admit that I'm 'loathe' to see you leave, Matthew. Truthfully, I got myself in such a pickle here I don't know what I'm going to do either."

"Then I must ask you about your family again," he said. "I do not know why you left the train, but can you reconsider and go to them now? I can purchase the fare for you. Do not concern yourself with that."

Sara shook her head. Her earlier foolish notions of trying to survive in Grand Forks, North Dakota, in the coming winter months had been foolish. She hadn't made it twenty-four hours in Kalispell, Montana, without being arrested. Even if she found an abandoned shack to live in, she had no idea what the laws were or if she would be arrested for loitering or vagrancy. And she didn't think she could survive without heat, even if she could find food.

"No, I can't," she said. She turned to him. He stood close, and she had to crane her head to look at him. "I lied about family in Grand Forks. I don't have any. My mother was the last of my family."

Matthew eyed her for a moment, then unexpectedly took one of her hands in his and brought it to his lips. The gesture sent a tingle through her arm, and her knees buckled for a moment.

"The look of despair in your eyes moves me, Miss Reed. Do not worry. I will take care of you."

Sara fought her way back from the spell of his blue eyes. She pulled her hand from his, not quite sure why Emily didn't want to marry him.

"As a modern woman, I should argue that I don't need to be taken care of, but I have to admit that sounds just about perfect right now," she said with a faint smile. "But only for a bit. I just need to figure a few things out."

"A modern woman," Matthew repeated with a lift of his lips. "Yes, you do appear to be quite progressive. Very well then. Until you 'figure a few things out,' as you say. How may I help?"

Sara, her knees still weak, thought it best to put some distance between Matthew and herself. She moved to reclaim her seat.

"I have no earthly idea right now. So much has happened today. I feel overwhelmed."

"Yes, of course you would," he said. "I will not press you further but will give you time to think. I can only stay in Kalispell a few days and then must return to Seattle. Perhaps you would like to return to Spokane?"

"I don't know," Sara said. "I just don't know."

"Very well. I think you must rest now," he said. "You look very tired."

Sara felt tired, but she knew she would never be able to sleep. She was too keyed up, had too much to think about. For the past two weeks, she'd done little else but dwell on the mysteries of time travel and why she had traveled in time. She had hoped and prayed that she would wake up in the twenty-first century, but with each passing day, that had seemed less likely.

Incarcerated as she had been with no idea how long she would remain in jail, Sara had spared herself the heartache of working on a plan to return to her own time. She knew it probably involved the train, but she didn't know how. Without knowing why she'd been thrown back in time, she had no idea how to travel forward.

"Can we take a walk?" she asked. "I mean, I can walk by myself if you're too tired, but I think I'd rather get out and get some fresh air."

"Certainly," Matthew said.

"Good," Sara said. She walked to the door, and Matthew cleared his throat and hesitated.

"What is it?"

"A hat perhaps? To cover your hair? I think it might be chilly outside. Perhaps your shawl?"

"Oh!" Sara exclaimed, running a quick hand to her hair. "Wait!" She ran into the bathroom, found the strip of red cotton she had ripped off her T-shirt and wrapped her hair on top of her head.

Self-consciously, she returned to the bedroom and rummaged in the boxes for the hat he had bought. She stepped over to the mirror above the dresser and settled the broad-brimmed, rose-ribboned velvet hat on her head, fumbling with the hatpin enclosed in the box. She winced as she stabbed her scalp, but she finally managed to secure the hat. She tilted her head to the left and right, but the hat seemed securely affixed to her bun.

Matthew picked up her shawl and set it around her shoulders. He held out his arm.

"Are you ready?"

"Yes," she said.

They walked down the stairs and into the lobby. Sara was pleased to see the lobby was empty.

"Good afternoon, sir, miss," Gerry said as they rounded the corner of the stairs. "How was your lunch?"

"Very good, thank you, Gerry. You can have someone pick the tray up now from Miss Reed's—from my sister's room."

Sara looked up quickly. Matthew's jaw tightened. He seemed annoyed at his slipup. She certainly understood, having her own lies to deal with.

"Sure," said Gerry.

"Oh, I am reminded," Matthew continued. "I need to send a telegram to Seattle. My parents will have expected my return and will worry."

"*Our* parents," Sara whispered out of the corner of her mouth.

"Our parents," Matthew corrected hastily.

"Sure! You can write down the message and the address, and I'll have the boy run it over to Walter at the train station to send out."

Sara jerked at the mention of Walter's name. Under her hand, she felt Matthew stiffen.

"Yes, that would be fine," he said. Releasing Sara's hand, Matthew took the paper Gerry handed him and scribbled some things down. He gave it back to Gerry, and he took Sara's hand under his arm again.

"As fast as they can send it, Gerry."

Gerry nodded. "I'll get the boy now."

Matthew nodded and led Sara out of the hotel.

"That got complicated," Sara said as they stepped outside into the golden light of the late autumn afternoon. The streets had settled somewhat as people probably started to head home for the evening. With her free hand, she pulled her shawl more tightly around her shoulders before tugging at her hat to make sure it was still secure.

"Yes, it did," Matthew said. "I never lie, so this is proving difficult for me."

"I'm sorry, Matthew," she said. She had tried never to lie either, but by necessity, she had been forced into it. She had no intention of announcing that she was some sort of time traveler, not in Matthew's time and not in her time, if she ever got back. Either era would see her medicated or locked up for observation.

He looked down at her with a lift of his lips. "That is not your fault, Miss Reed, but the dictates of society. There was little way for me to help you either on the train or here if I did not claim a familial relationship with you."

Sara heard a gasp and swung around to see Mrs. Feeney standing on the boardwalk, several other ladies at her side. The shocked expressions on their faces made it obvious that they had heard Matthew's words.

CHAPTER THIRTEEN

"Mr. Webster, had I known when you attempted to bribe me into dropping the charges against this woman that she was *not* your sister, I would never have entered into the agreement!"

Instinctively, Matthew set Miss Reed behind him to shield her from the vituperation in Mrs. Feeney's face and words. He thought quickly but felt quite inept at lying. Nevertheless, he must do so for Miss Reed's sake.

"I am not certain what you think you overheard, Mrs. Feeney, but you were well compensated for the trouble *my sister* caused you. I did not *attempt* to bribe you. I *succeeded*, and your husband prepared the document to prove it."

A rage such as Matthew had never known took hold of him at the censure on the women's faces. Clearly, Mrs. Feeney had not desisted in spreading gossip about Miss Reed.

"If there is nothing further, you *will* excuse us." He pulled Miss Reed close to his side as he stormed past the sputtering face of Mrs. Feeney and her gaggle of wide-eyed female friends.

Miss Reed kept pace with him silently until, his anger spent, he slowed. He turned down a street and came to a halt to gaze down upon her.

"Forgive me, Miss Reed. Truly. I cannot believe that I dragged you down the street so unceremoniously. I do not know what overcame me."

Slightly winded, her cheeks were red from exertion. She adjusted her hat and smiled tentatively.

"That was pretty brutal back there," she said. "I'm guessing I won't be settling down in Kalispell, that's for sure."

"I think not," he agreed. "Had you thought about staying here?"

Miss Reed surveyed the street and shook her head. "No, I guess not." She returned her gaze to his face. "What did you bribe her with, by the way? And what was this about a document?"

"I am a businessman first and foremost, Miss Reed," he said with a smile. "I never conduct business without proper documentation. I offered Mrs. Feeney a sum for her troubles, and she accepted. That is all."

"How much of a sum?" she pressed. "I intend to pay you back someday, if I can. So, how much?"

Matthew took her hand under his arm and prepared to resume their walk, albeit at a more leisurely pace. Miss Reed resisted and crossed her arms over her stomach.

"How much?" she insisted.

"Mrs. Feeney accepted a shopping trip to Seattle at my expense," Matthew said with reluctance. "Although in hindsight, perhaps I should have sent her on a trip to Chicago. I do not wish to think what gossip she might spread in Seattle."

"A shopping trip to Seattle? With hotel, no doubt? Good gravy, Matthew, how much did that cost? Certainly more than the skirt, blouse and the price of her anger."

Matthew shook his head. He had been prepared to pay much more for Miss Reed's release, much more.

"It is nothing, really, but as I said before, I also regret that I did not include a nondisclosure agreement. I really should have. I thought Mrs. Feeney might conduct herself as a lady, but I can see that I was wrong. I have not done well by you."

Miss Reed reached out a hand and laid it on his chest.

"Oh, yes, you have, Matthew. You have most certainly done well by me. I can never thank you enough."

Matthew covered her hand with his own. A shock went through his hand at the contact, a delightful tingle that seemed to run up his arm and into his chest.

They stared at each other for a moment, and Matthew lost himself in the golden flecks of her brown eyes. His heartbeat slowed, and his breathing grew shallow. Time stood still, and he willed the moment to continue.

Miss Reed drew in a deep breath and blinked. She pulled her hand from under his with a shaky laugh.

"Shall we try our walk again? Or should I return to the room and hide out there until I manage to get out of town? I feel like I'm in high school all over again."

"Hold your head high, Miss Reed," Matthew said softly. "Do not let them best you—not those women and not your memories."

She smiled then, a breathtakingly bright smile that warmed his heart and brought a lump to his throat.

"Well then, let's finish our walk," she said as she tucked her hand under his arm.

They explored the town on foot for the next hour until Matthew felt Miss Reed lagging. She seemed remarkably inept with her skirts, tripping over them often, though the length appeared appropriate. He wondered again at her origins and the long johns in which she first appeared.

Matthew guided her back toward the hotel, hoping that Mrs. Feeney and her posse had moved on. On their return to the hotel, he delivered her to her room to rest until dinnertime.

"Do you mind if I eat dinner in my room?" she asked as she dropped into a chair in less than genteel fashion. He waited just inside the door.

"Not at all," Matthew said. "Shall I join you?"

"Do you want to?" she asked. "I don't mind, but you might be more comfortable dining in the restaurant. The desk isn't the best substitute for a dining table."

His appetite restored, Matthew smiled.

"I quite enjoyed our private meal. Let us eat here. In the meantime, I must make arrangements for train passage. Have you decided if you want to return to Spokane or... Do you have a home there?"

She shook her head. "No."

Matthew still had many questions for Miss Reed, but he hesitated to press her.

"Shall I book passage to Seattle then?"

She looked up at him. Her bemused expression gave him the answer he needed. No matter what her words, he knew what he must do.

"I will book passage to Seattle. You will return with me."

Her knuckles whitened as she clasped her hands together.

"What will I do there? Where will I stay?"

"You will stay at my house. My parents will welcome you." Privately, Matthew was in some doubt about his mother's reception, but he hoped for the best.

"Are you sure? Just for a while. Really!"

"For as long as you need, Miss Reed. Now, you must rest."

Matthew left and went downstairs to speak to Gerry.

"Gerry, I need two tickets on tomorrow's train to Seattle," he said. "Two private compartments in first class." He laid some money on the counter.

"Certainly, sir. I'll send the boy to buy those for you. I'm sorry to hear you are leaving so soon."

"My sister is not well. I think I need to get her to Seattle to see our physician as soon as possible."

"Oh, I *am* sorry to hear that, sir."

Matthew nodded.

"Please have dinner for two sent to her room in two hours," he said. "She is resting at the moment."

"Yes, of course."

"Thank you, Gerry."

Matthew returned to his own room to pace. He did not normally rest during the day and could not do so now, especially given the underlying current of tension that ran through him.

He had no idea what his parents' reception of Miss Reed might be. He imagined his father would greet her with his usual impeccable manners, as would his mother. His mother, however, would most certainly question his decision to bring Miss Reed home, and Matthew had no concrete explanation to offer her regarding the origin of Miss Reed's troubles.

She was still unwilling to discuss the events that led her to take shelter in his compartment on the train, or what instinct prompted her to leave the train without reaching her destination. She had only confused him further by revealing that she had no family in Grand Forks, and he assumed that had not been her final destination. In fact, she seemed to have had no particular destination at all when boarding the train.

Regarding her eccentricities—her odd clothing, the careless grooming of her hair, even her casual speech—he did not know what to make of those either. Matthew had spent enough time in Spokane to know that the residents dressed, behave and spoke with no significant difference than did the residents of Seattle.

It was almost as if Miss Reed had been dropped from the sky, or more whimsically, had fallen from a nest, perhaps an eagle's nest, given the golden flecks in her eyes.

Matthew snorted. Foolish notions. He was not often given to flights of the imagination, priding himself on being a practical man, but the mystery of Miss Reed tested the boundaries of pragmatism. In short, she was an enigma, and he was determined to solve the puzzle.

Following two hours of pacing and ruminating, Matthew presented himself at Miss Reed's door. The food had already been delivered, and he bent to pick up the tray, thinking himself fortunate to have found another skill as a waiter should his businesses fail and his family fortune vanish in some unprecedented disaster.

He balanced the tray in one hand and knocked on her door with the other.

"Matthew?" she asked in a low voice.

"Yes, bearing food."

She opened the door and stood back to let him in. Her cheeks glowed, and he suspected that she blushed. Of course, it was quite irregular for him to dine in her room, but it was her wish, and he did not blame her for needing privacy after her ordeal of the past few weeks. The encounter only hours ago with Mrs. Feeney served only to add more turmoil to an already difficult situation. He wished them well away from Kalispell.

He set the tray down on the desk as before. Several lamps had been lit to ward off the darkness that had now descended.

"Were you able to rest?" he asked.

"Yes, I slept a little," she said, raising a hand to smooth her hair, which did appear to have a tousled look about it. Under the lamplight, her hair glowed with a reddish-brown tint.

He pulled the chair out from the desk for her, and she sat. He took the other available chair.

"I have asked Gerry to book train fare to Seattle tomorrow. If I remember correctly, the train will leave at eleven in the morning."

Miss Reed looked up quickly.

"I'll have to see Walter again, won't I?" she said. "He was so disappointed in me. I let him down."

"I think it is largely unavoidable," Matthew said. "I can certainly present our tickets, and perhaps he will be too preoccupied with other passengers to take notice of you, but you do run the risk of being seen."

She sighed heavily and toyed with her food. He berated himself for raising a subject that undermined her appetite. She looked frail.

"It's just as well. I need to apologize to him," she said.

Matthew knew a moment's pride in her. He too would have sought to make amends to someone he had wronged, however much in need he might have been.

"I should probably apologize to Mrs. Feeney before I go," she added. "Maybe I can stop by her house in the morning and see her."

Matthew stiffened. No, perhaps he would not have made amends to just anyone.

"While I commend your desire to make amends to the station agent, I do not think it is wise to visit Mrs. Feeney, Miss Reed. I think that will do you more harm than good."

"She does seem to hold a grudge, doesn't she?" Miss Reed stated. "I would take it back if I could, not stolen the clothing, but I thought my...uh...long johns would shock a few people. I don't know what I was thinking at the time, but I thought the luggage was abandoned. I don't know why I thought that."

"It is done," Matthew said, "and cannot be undone. Mrs. Feeney has been handsomely compensated. Please do not distress yourself further on her account."

Miss Reed nodded but continued to toy with her food.

"Please eat, Miss Reed. You must regain your strength. The change in your appearance over the past two weeks is dramatic."

She glanced up quickly, raising a hand to pat her hair.

"What do you mean?"

Matthew's face flamed. One did not normally comment on a woman's appearance other than to compliment her.

"You have lost too much weight," he said quietly. "You look as if a strong breeze might topple you over."

"Oh!" she said with a faint smile. "That! Yes, I noticed." She shrugged. "Weight loss is a good thing, isn't it? Something we all strive for?"

Matthew frowned. "Not that I am aware of," he said. "To lose weight normally suggests that one is ill or under great duress."

"Well, most of us are trying to lose weight all the time. *I've* been trying to lose weight, so this is actually a good thing." She patted her midriff.

Matthew looked at her dubiously. "I cannot feel that is healthy," he said.

"Well, it wouldn't be if *you* lost weight," she said. "You're already in great shape just the way you are."

As if she suddenly heard her words, her cheeks colored.

Matthew was certain his own face matched the color of her now rosy cheeks.

"Why, thank you, Miss Reed!" Emboldened, he added, "I also thought you quite attractive when we first met and see no need for you to alter your physical appearance any further than the past two weeks of deprivation have already done," he said.

They smiled at each other, Matthew feeling as shy as a schoolboy. Miss Reed picked up her fork and began to eat.

CHAPTER FOURTEEN

"There he is," Sara said the following morning as she spotted Walter on the platform of the train station.

"I will await you just over there, Miss Reed," Matthew said, pointing to one end of the platform. "I intend to keep a close eye on you, so if you need me for any reason, signal."

"I'll be fine, Matthew. Thank you."

Matthew moved away, and Sara approached Walter, who had not yet seen her.

"Hello, Walter. Can I talk to you for a second?" Sara asked.

The tall man, in the act of checking his pocket watch, turned and looked down at her with surprise.

"Miss Reed!" he exclaimed. "You're out of jail!"

Sara cringed as she looked around at the passengers standing nearby. Fortunately, none seemed to hear him.

"Ummm...yeah," she said. "I wanted to apologize, Walter. I know you gave me a chance when I first got here, and I betrayed you. I'm so sorry," she said.

The train hissed as it slowed, and Walter cast a quick glance toward it before turning his attention back to her. He shrugged.

"I don't know what happened to make you do something like that, Miss Reed, but I hope everything has been resolved. Did they drop the charges? I really hated to see you go to jail over some silly clothes, but there was nothing I could do. I can't tell you how bad I've felt for you."

Sara nodded. "Mr.—my brother came to my rescue, thank goodness, and persuaded Mrs. Feeney to drop the charges. I can't tell you why I did what I did. I can only say that I'm truly sorry, and I appreciate the chance you gave me."

"Well, you were shaping up to be a great clerk," he said. "It's just a shame you had to..." He didn't finish his sentence, for which Sara was grateful. "Where are you off to?" He looked over at Matthew, who tipped his hat in Walter's direction.

"Seattle," she said.

Walter nodded. "Good luck, Miss Reed."

"Thank you, Walter."

He hurried away to greet the conductor, and Sara turned toward Matthew.

Tall, slender and elegant in his derby and a long dark-gray overcoat, he smiled encouragingly as she walked toward him. Sara drew in a deep breath to steady herself on weak knees—weak not because of her encounter with Walter, but because of the handsome man who watched her approach.

He held out his arm as she neared, and she tucked her hand underneath it as if she'd been doing so all her life.

"Did it go well?"

"Reasonably well," she said. "He knows I'm sorry and that I feel awful about what I did. That's all I could say. He accepted the apology."

"Good," Matthew said. "Now, perhaps you may leave all this unpleasantness behind."

Sara didn't respond. Apologizing to Walter was the least of her troubles. She was still stuck in the early twentieth century, far from anything she knew.

"Come along, Ronald. The train is already here!"

Sara swung around to the sound of Mrs. Feeney's voice. The short woman emerged from the station with her husband in tow.

"Oh, no!" Sara whispered hoarsely. "What now?"

Matthew let out a short curse. "What now, indeed. I do not believe Mrs. Feeney pursues you inasmuch as I think she is boarding the train for the trip to Seattle I awarded her."

Mrs. Feeney, carrying a small satchel, marched onto the platform, while her husband struggled through the door with several larger bags in hand. A porter followed them with two large suitcases in a cart.

Having not yet seen Sara, Mrs. Feeney moved to the edge of the platform where the conductor and Walter engaged in conversation. Even from where she stood, Sara could see Walter eye Mrs. Feeney in surprise. He looked over the woman's head to where she and Matthew stood.

Matthew grabbed Sara's hand.

"Come!" he said. They leapt aboard the front end of the car, and Matthew hurried down the corridor with Sara firmly in hand.

"Here!" he said. He pulled open a compartment door and guided her inside, turning to lock the door and pull the curtains on the door. He crossed the room to close the curtains on the platform side of the train.

"It is possible we can reach Seattle without an unpleasant encounter, but I think it highly unlikely that we can avoid Mrs. Feeney altogether," he said as he removed his hat and stowed it on an overhead rack. "However, the longer we can delay the inevitable, the more pleasant our journey will be."

He shook his head. "I cannot tell you how sorry I am that I did not find a way to silence the infernal woman, or at least send her to Chicago."

"You couldn't know she'd take the first train to Seattle," Sara said as she removed her hat. Matthew stowed her hat and the dark dark-blue coat he had bought for her on the rack alongside his hat. Her yoga pants, T-shirt and fleece jacket unsalvageable, she had thrown them away.

"No," Matthew agreed.

Sara sat down on a bench next to the window opposite the platform. She moved the curtains aside and looked out over several wooden buildings that appeared to be warehouses. Several other tracks lay between the train and the buildings. The view was largely industrial and not particularly attractive.

She returned her attention to the compartment. Matthew had taken a seat across from her and perused the same sight as she had.

"How long is the trip to Seattle?" she asked.

"About twenty hours if all goes well. We should arrive tomorrow at about eight o'clock in the morning."

Sara quirked an eyebrow.

"Are we both sleeping in this compartment?"

Matthew's lips twitched. "I did try to book two compartments, but the train is full, and I could only book one. I think I will *not* take a berth in the tourist coach again in case some further mishap should befall you. I realize this is most peculiar and that you might feel uncomfortable with my presence in the night, but I assure you, I mean you no harm. I will stretch out on this bench while you sleep. I hope that agrees with you."

Sara returned his smile.

"That's fine with me," she said, "as long as you're comfortable with it."

"I am more comfortable sitting on this bench all night rather than worry about where you might disappear to again."

"I won't take off again, I promise," Sara said.

"I am glad to hear it."

A sharp voice in the hallway caught their attention, and they looked at each other. Mrs. Feeney's voice carried.

"Come along, Ronald," she said. "I think now that I should have left you at home and invited Gladys to come with me."

Sara clapped a hand to her mouth to stifle a laugh, but Matthew chuckled outright, a rich, deep-throated sound that warmed Sara's heart.

"I pity that poor man," Matthew said. "She is a most unpleasant woman. I do not wish to bring up an uncomfortable subject, but could you not have rummaged through someone else's luggage? Anyone else?"

Before she could help herself, Sara snorted in the middle of her laugh. She dropped her hand.

"How I wish!" she said. "I'm almost glad to know that I'm not the only one she yells at. Almost. But I feel sorry for him, too." She continued. "You know, I'm not stepping foot out there until we get to Seattle. So, if there's food to eat or coffee to drink, the porter will have to bring it to me."

"Yes, I think that would be wise," Matthew said. "I did so hope to leave all that behind. I am not used to skulking about in this manner."

"Are we skulking?" Sara asked with a grin.

"Most definitely," he said. "You with good reason, and me because I am cowed by a small woman with a sharp tongue." He looked as if he was only half kidding.

"Oh, I think you're avoiding her for me, Matthew. I doubt that you're one bit afraid of her."

"You would be surprised, Miss Reed. A few words of gossip can destroy a person's reputation, and I worry that she will continue in her quest to ruin yours."

"So, you're worried about me, not yourself."

He shrugged.

"I am a man. I can withstand that sort of thing. Such is not the case for a lady. To be ostracized is a lonely thing."

"You forget I've lived that way much of my life. A lot of 'good people' looked down on my mother and me. I don't care about reputations."

He pressed his lips together. "Yes, of course. I spoke without thinking. We will not worry about it for the moment."

"Do you think we'll actually run into Mrs. Feeney after we get to Seattle? It's a big city, right?"

"My family is quite prominent," Matthew said. "Mrs. Feeney would know where to find me if she chose."

Sara nodded, chewing on her lower lip.

"If that's true, then at some point, she'll find out for certain that I'm not your sister. I think you confused her yesterday, but once we reach

Seattle, things will change. I hardly think your parents are going to adopt me." Sara laughed without mirth.

"Yes, I am not certain how to approach that," he said, "but I must." He smiled as if he thought of something. "My father, however, would adopt you without question. He has always wanted a daughter. He thought it would be Emily."

Sara tried not to wince. She really didn't like Emily—and she didn't even know the girl.

Matthew's face sobered on his last words, and Sara disliked Emily even more. Why on earth didn't the girl want to marry him? He was handsome, charming, kind, thoughtful, intelligent, generous and wealthy, from the sound of it. What wasn't to like?

"Her loss," Sara muttered.

Matthew looked up quickly. The corner of his mouth twitched.

"You tease me, I think, Miss Reed."

"Oh, no, not at all. I truly believe that."

His cheeks bronzed, and he looked away.

"I am flattered that you think so, Miss Reed. Thank you."

Sara would have loved to drop the subject, to avoid reminding him of Emily, but some perverse imp made her continue.

"Maybe now that she's had some time to think about your proposal, she'll reconsider."

Matthew threw her a sideways look.

"I sincerely doubt it. As I mentioned before, Emily rarely changes her mind once she makes a decision."

"I don't really understand why she would turn you down," Sara said, voicing her earlier thoughts.

Matthew crossed and recrossed his legs restlessly.

"Because she does not love me?"

Sara shook her head. "That seems hard to believe. Is there someone else?"

Matthew drew in a sharp breath and leaned forward to peer through the curtains.

"Not that I am aware of," he said without looking at her.

A whistle and hiss of steam heralded the train's departure, and Sara pulled the curtains wide to watch the train move away from the station.

"I'm sorry," Sara said. "I didn't mean to suggest something you hadn't thought of."

He leaned back against his bench and faced her.

"I have thought of every possibility for Emily's rejection of my proposal, Miss Reed, including that she had met someone and did not tell me. I find it hard to believe that to be the case, however, as she normally tells me everything. And her parents would have known and told my parents. No, I believe it is simply that she does not see me as a husband but merely a childhood friend."

Sara watched myriad emotions cross his face, from sadness to confusion to regret. Her heart ached for him. She dropped the subject and stared out the window at the passing scenery of evergreen trees interspersed with the gold and red fall foliage of deciduous trees.

"When do we reach Spokane?" she asked.

Matthew, who had been staring out of the window as well, looked at her sharply.

"If I remember correctly, at about 6:30 this evening. Why do you ask? I thought we had agreed you would continue on to Seattle?"

"Oh, I am. I really wouldn't know anyone in Spokane—I mean, I don't know anyone in Spokane."

"So, you are not thinking of disappearing from the train when we reach Spokane?" he asked dubiously.

"No, I was just wondering what time we got there." In fact, Sara wondered what Spokane looked like in nineteen hundred. Six o'clock was late though, given that the fall days were short. It would be dark when they arrived.

She had been truthful in saying she hadn't planned on disappearing when they reached Spokane, but now that Matthew had raised the issue, she gave it some serious thought. She smiled brightly in his direction and looked out the window as she ruminated.

There could be nothing for her in Spokane. No school, no apartment, not even her mother. She'd gone too far back in time for that. She would end up begging on the streets like so many people seemed to do now, and probably with much less success and a lot more danger.

Her best bet right now was to stick with Matthew...like a leech. At least that's what she felt like, but her one effort at independence had gone horribly wrong, and she couldn't face another mistake like that. She couldn't imagine what Matthew's parents would say when he arrived with some strange woman in tow, but she trusted that he knew them and knew what to expect.

A knock on the door startled both of them. Matthew rose and opened the door a crack.

"Excuse me, sir. I need to check your tickets." Sara could just barely see a porter standing outside their door.

Matthew reached into his coat pocket and produced their tickets.

"Mr. Webster and Miss Reed," the porter said. "What time would you like to dine?"

"About six o'clock," Matthew said. "But we would like a tray delivered to the compartment, please. My sister is not feeling well enough to venture out to the dining room. Could you bring some coffee in the meantime?"

"Yes, sir. Right away." The porter appeared to scribble something on paper before turning away. Matthew peered into the hallway before shutting and locking the door again.

"Six o'clock, huh?" Sara asked. "Are you trying to make sure I have to make the decision whether to stay and eat or get off in Spokane hungry?"

Matthew's lips parted into a handsome wide smile. "Well, yes, Miss Reed. That *is* what I intended."

Sara responded to his smile and hoped he hadn't realized that she had contemplated the latter. She wasn't sure what the future held, or even the coming days, but she knew she didn't want to see the last of Matthew Webster's smile.

CHAPTER FIFTEEN

Hours later, Matthew awoke from a doze. A glance out of the window revealed night had fallen, and he checked his pocket watch. Five thirty. Darkness came so early in the fall.

He raised his eyes and studied Miss Reed's face as she napped on the opposite bench. Settled on her side with her cheek against the pillow and lower limbs drawn to her chest, she looked quite childlike.

Normally a man of temperate emotions, Matthew had no experience with the tumultuous emotions such as he had experienced over the past two weeks, from his grief at Emily's rejection to the surprising fervency with which he sought to protect Miss Reed from whatever mysterious bad fortune had befallen her.

She stirred, and he rose to pull her blanket higher onto her shoulders. Her eyes opened, and she sat up hastily.

"Where are we?" she asked.

"If we are on schedule, I think we must be in Idaho, about a half hour from Spokane. I am sorry to awaken you. Your blanket had slipped off your shoulders, and I thought you might be cold."

She clutched the blanket to her stomach.

"Thank you," she said. "I'm starved. What time is dinner again?"

"I ordered it for six o'clock."

"Oh, that's right. So I don't think about getting off the train."

Matthew responded to her smile with one of his own but said nothing.

Miss Reed rose and stretched with a languorous arching of her back and extension of her arms out to the sides. Matthew eyed the movement appreciatively but looked away discreetly when she turned to look at him.

"Is there any chance we can go for a walk or something? On the train? Can we go from car to car?"

Matthew rose. "Yes, of course. I thought you might not wish to encounter Mrs. Feeney, so I did not suggest it."

"I don't want to, but I feel a little bit cooped up in here," she said.

"Come, let us stroll," he said. He opened the door and peered out, but no one was in sight. He pulled the door open wider and allowed her to precede him.

"Which way?" she said in a whisper as if she worried about being overheard.

"To the right," he said. "I believe the dining car is next and then the observation car."

"You lead," she said.

Matthew stepped in front of her and made his way down the narrow corridor, stopping often to see that Miss Reed followed. They reached the end of the car, and he pushed open the door.

Miss Reed stared at the vestibule.

"I'd forgotten about that," she murmured.

He cocked his head. "Are you frightened, Miss Reed? Come, take my hand."

She slipped her hand into his, and Matthew led her through the rather chilly and noisy vestibule and into the dining car. At 5:30, the dining room was already full of passengers, merrily talking and eating. Waiters moved up and down the aisle serving dinner.

Miss Reed hesitated just inside the doorway and pulled her hand from his. Matthew turned.

"Do you want to return to the compartment?"

She shook her head.

"No, I just have to run the gauntlet, right?"

Matthew smiled. "I suppose one could look at it that way. If I were alone, I would simply follow the maître d' to my seat, smiling and nodding along the way. I do not think of it as a gauntlet." He turned and surveyed the dining room with fresh eyes.

"No, you wouldn't," she said. "You *belong* here. I'm pretty sure everyone will be staring at me as I pass through." She mumbled, almost as if to herself.

"But I cannot imagine why, Miss Reed. No one here knows of your past, of the unfortunate incident in Kalispell. With the exception of the Feeneys, and I do not see them here."

Miss Reed blinked as if in a reverie and met his eyes. "That's true," she said. She looked down at her skirt and smoothed it before reaching a hand to her hair. "No one knows," she repeated.

She reached for his hand. Matthew was touched by the trusting gesture. Normally, a man would offer a woman his arm in public, not hold her hand in such an intimate gesture, but he submitted happily.

They moved through the dining room and entered into the observation car. A porter, carrying a tray of coffee, paused and greeted them.

"Good evening, sir, ma'am. Can I get you something? We're pretty busy tonight."

"No, thank you," Matthew said. "We're just strolling."

"Very good, sir." The porter turned away and moved down the corridor.

Sara remembered the layout of the observation car, but she was fascinated to see it when she wasn't as panicked as she had been the first time.

Matthew led the way down the corridor, past several compartments, a card room, the porter's kitchen, and into the large observation lounge. Comfortable easy chairs lined either side of the car, notable for large plate glass picture windows, the majority of which were now curtained. Several passengers sat at writing desks tucked against the walls. The lounge bustled with passengers, leaving no available chairs.

This time no one stared at her or her clothing.

"The porter was right. They *are* busy in here this evening," Matthew said.

"That's okay. We have the compartment. I'm sure dinner will be there soon."

"Are you ready to return?"

Miss Reed nodded.

They retraced their steps and arrived at the compartment in time to feel the slowing of the train and to hear the requisite whistle as it neared the outskirts of Spokane.

The porter arrived with their food in minutes.

"Thank you, George," Matthew said as the porter set the tray down on a side table. "Are we on time for Spokane?"

"How do you know all their names?" Miss Reed asked. "And why are all the porters named George?"

Matthew smiled.

"I do not know all their names. All porters are referred to as 'George,' a reference to 'George Pullman,' the inventor and builder of the sleeper compartments."

"Oh, that's funny," Miss Reed said, biting into her food, and Matthew was pleased to see her appetite had returned.

As they ate, the train slowed further, and the lights of Spokane came into view. Miss Reed stopped eating and stared out of the window with a look of what Matthew could only call consternation on her face.

"Does something trouble you, Miss Reed?" he asked. His heart pounded, and he set his own food aside. Was she going to announce that she was leaving the train? He was not ready to say good-bye to her. He still had so many unasked questions, so much that he did not understand about her.

She continued to stare out of the window, almost pressing her face against it.

"No," she said, though her tone belied her denial. "I just didn't realize that Spokane was so big in nineteen hundred."

"Did you not?" he asked, somewhat relieved that her words presaged no immediate departure on her part.

She glanced at him, then back to the window with a shake of her head.

"No, not really."

She said no more, and Matthew refrained from asking further questions. Her actions and words suggested she had never been on a train before, certainly not one that had pulled into Spokane, but how was that possible, given that he had first found her on the train upon its departure from Spokane?

The train slowed further and came to a stop in front of the station. Matthew watched Miss Reed out of the corner of his eye. He could not possibly stop her if she wanted to detrain in Spokane. That was her right, but he fervently hoped she would travel on to Seattle with him.

She rose hastily, and his heart dropped to his stomach. He forced himself to remain seated.

"I'm just going to go out for a minute while we're here. Can you come with me?"

Matthew jumped up with alacrity. "Yes, certainly."

"You thought I was going to take off, didn't you?" she asked as she pulled her shawl around her shoulders. Matthew noted she eschewed her hat.

"I am afraid that I did," Matthew said, donning his overcoat and hat. "I do not think it is quite proper for me to concern myself with your activities, but the truth is, I do."

He let out a deep breath at his confession.

Miss Reed slipped her hand under his arm.

"I'm not going anywhere, I promise. I don't have anywhere to go. I just want to see the station."

Matthew nodded and tucked her hand against his side as he opened the door and led her out of the compartment. They stepped down to the platform and the chill of a brisk fall night, joining other passengers who descended to take advantage of the respite from the confines of the train.

Matthew had thought Miss Reed desired a stroll, but she seemed frozen in place, staring at the monumental two-story brick building, much larger than the modest train depot in Seattle.

"It's the same one!" she exclaimed.

"I beg your pardon?" Matthew asked.

She threw him a quick look.

"Oh, nothing. I'm just mumbling."

"Rather cryptically, I must say." Matthew could not resist commenting.

Miss Reed pulled her hand from his arm and laced her fingers together tightly. Matthew instantly regretted his words.

"I apologize, Miss Reed. I did not mean to cause offense," he said.

"And I apologize for blurting out what must seem like random odd comments. I really do. I wish I could explain, but I can't."

"I understand," Matthew said. He wished he did, but he did not.

As if she could read his mind, Miss Reed said, "I doubt it, but thanks for saying so anyway."

She reached for his arm again, and he closed his hands over hers as if he could keep her there. He had the worst fear, however, that he could not.

A furious whisper caught his ear, and he turned to see the tight face of Mrs. Feeney, standing nearby with her husband. Before turning his back on them to shield Miss Reed from their view, Matthew nodded to the poor man, who had the grace to look embarrassed.

"I cannot believe...she..." The higher pitches of Mrs. Feeney's voice carried. "No amount of money..."

He could not, however, prevent Miss Reed from hearing Mrs. Feeney's words, and she peered around him to see the commotion.

"Come, let us return to the compartment before I lose my temper," he said.

"Oh, man, don't do that," Miss Reed murmured. "I'm sure that will only make things worse. Right now, no one is listening to her but her husband, and he looks like he wishes he were a hundred miles away."

"I am sure that he does." He escorted Miss Reed back onto the train and to the safety of the compartment. He pulled the curtains shut, as they opened up to the station.

"I really must do something about her," Matthew said with a frown as he removed his coat and hat. "I cannot have her spreading gossip all over Seattle."

"I don't see what you could do to stop her," Miss Reed said in a tight voice. She laced and unlaced her fingers together in her lap.

"I will think of something," he said. "I promise."

Matthew retook his seat, and they sat without speaking until the train left the station. Matthew had many questions he wished he could ask, but it behooved him to remain silent.

"I think I'll get some sleep," Miss Reed said. "I don't know why I feel so tired."

"You have had a difficult few weeks. I am not surprised that you are tired," Matthew said. "I will resume my doze as well."

She nodded and lay down on the bench, pulling the blanket over her lower limbs. Matthew stretched out his legs and crossed his arms.

"Will you be warm enough without a blanket?" she asked.

"Yes, I am fine, thank you." He smiled. She closed her eyes, and he followed suit, letting his cares dissipate for the moment. A sense of relaxation stole over him and he slipped into sleep.

CHAPTER SIXTEEN

A sudden lurch in the train awakened Sara, and she opened her eyes. The bench opposite her was empty, and she pushed herself upright hastily. The tangled mess at her ankles indicated she was still dressed in long skirts. But where was Matthew?

"Matthew?" she called out. The compartment lights were still on as they had been when she fell asleep. Matthew didn't respond. She rose and tapped on the washroom door. She supposed she could have waited until he came out, but somehow she couldn't make herself wait.

"Matthew? Are you in there?"

No answer.

The hard knot in Sara's stomach, never really far away, tightened painfully.

"Matthew?" she called out to nowhere in particular. He wasn't in the compartment. His overnight case, hat and coat were on the overhead rack. He hadn't been a figment of her imagination.

Still, she couldn't ignore the feeling of panic that his disappearance caused. She pulled open the door and ran into the hallway, looking to the right and to the left. No Matthew.

She turned right and hurried down the corridor. Maybe he'd gone to the dining room to get something to eat. She had no idea what time it was.

Sara pulled open the door to the vestibule and, without fear this time, ran through the connector and pushed open the door to the dining car.

She stopped short. The dining room was in near darkness, with the exception of several sconces that provided a dim light. Her heart dropped to join the knot in her stomach.

"Matthew?" she whispered, though she knew he wasn't in the

darkened room. She ran the length of the car and hurried into the observation car. Similarly lit, it seemed as if the passengers had gone back to their compartments to sleep. What time was it anyway? she wondered. She moved down the corridor, peeping into the card room and the porters' kitchen. She tiptoed past the closed compartments, not wanting to disturb anyone sleeping. She reached the end of the car and found the observation lounge empty.

Her breath came quickly, both from running and from anxiety. Where on earth was Matthew?

She turned and ran back through the cars, reaching her compartment without seeing even a porter. As she reached for the door, Matthew appeared at the opposite end of the corridor.

Her heart leapt with joy. She hadn't imagined him! He hadn't disappeared!

"Where have you been?" she hissed. Matthew put a finger to his lips and approached. He guided her into the compartment.

"I woke up and you were gone. I couldn't find you anywhere!" she babbled, turning to face him. She planted a hand on his chest.

Matthew looked down in surprise as he took her hand in his. He placed a kiss into the palm and released it. Sara stared at her hand in stunned silence.

"I awakened and, restless, I decided to stroll through the adjoining cars. I think I hoped to speak to Mr. and Mrs. Feeney, but the hour was too late for a social call."

Sara pressed her hand to her face in bemusement. "What time is it?"

Matthew pulled his pocket watch out and consulted it. "Ten o'clock."

"I looked for you in the dining car and the observation lounge, but those are shut down."

"I am sorry, Miss Reed. I did not mean to worry you. I strolled in the opposite direction. It was not so long ago that we could not travel from car to car. I enjoy the modernity of the ease with which we can traverse the cars now, given the vestibules."

"Well, you scared me!" she said, growing unexpectedly angry.

"I am sorry," he said again. His smile though was unrepentant. "I truly did not mean to frighten you, but perhaps you can imagine how I felt when you disappeared from the train two weeks ago."

Sara shook her head. "It's not the same. I can't explain it, but it is *really* not the same."

Matthew sat down and crossed his legs.

"How is it different?"

Sara sank to her bench and clutched the blanket to her chest. She longed to confess everything to him, to share her nightmare with someone she trusted, but she couldn't bring herself to do so. He would think she was crazy.

She shook her head but pressed her lips together.

Matthew leaned forward.

"I know there is something about you, Miss Reed, that is...unusual. Why can you not confide in me? Have I not proven myself trustworthy?"

She bit into her bottom lip and shook her head.

"I wish you would just call me Sara," she said by way of distracting him.

Matthew blinked and sat back with a widening smile.

"As you know, it is only proper for me to call you Miss Reed, but I can call you Sara in private if you prefer," he said. "Can you not tell me what secret you harbor, Sara?"

At the intimate sound of her voice on his lips, Sara almost gave in and told him everything. Maybe the off-putting and more formal Miss Reed was better.

She shook her head. "No, I can't. Can we change the subject?"

Matthew sobered, drew in a deep breath and let it out slowly. "Yes, we can."

"Tell me about your childhood," she said.

He smiled gently, as if he understood her tactic.

"I do not think there is much to tell. I am an only child, as you know. I mentioned that my parents spoiled me, especially my mother. Emily was my childhood playmate. We attended school together as small children, but she attended a girl's high school, and I attended a boy's high school. I graduated from the University of Washington with a degree in business, as did Emily. My father inherited several financial institutions from his father, and I took over the business when my father decided that a life of leisure suited him more than working." He smiled with affection as he spoke of his father.

"Your life sounds very stable...safe," Sara said. She heard the envy in her voice and hoped that Matthew didn't.

He nodded. "Yes, I believe so. Stable is an apt description. Even safe. In general, I would characterize my life as stable. There have been few surprises." He eyed her pensively. "With the exception of the past few weeks, that is."

Sara nodded sympathetically. "You mean Emily."

He nodded. "Emily. And you, Sara. *You* have been quite a surprise."

Sara's heart jumped, but more with anxiety than pleasure at a perceived compliment. She worried about his inference.

"You're not suggesting that your stable life has become...unstable because of me, are you, Matthew? I wouldn't want that. I would *never* want that!" She shook her head emphatically.

He hesitated to answer, and Sara fidgeted in her seat. Well, yes, of course his life had been momentarily disrupted because of her, but nowhere near as much as it would be if he knew who...or what she really was.

"Unstable, no," he said with a shake of his head. "Infinitely more complex and interesting, yes."

"But not for long, Matthew. I promise. I'll try to get out of your hair as soon as I can, and you can continue with that wonderful-sounding stable life of yours." She tried to smile, but her lips felt crooked.

He leaned forward and took one of her hands in his.

"Please do not worry yourself so, Sara. You need not concern yourself with 'getting out of my hair.' I have come to believe over the past few days that a complex and interesting life is much more...well, *interesting* than the fairly routine life I have been living. If I am to be honest, I feel you have more surprises in store for me, and short of endangering yourself or others, I look forward to discovering what those may be."

Against her will, Sara laced her fingers through his and gripped his hand tightly, on the verge of disclosing her "surprises." She opened her mouth to speak, and he raised her hand to his lips again, pressing a kiss on the back. She could think of nothing else besides the warm touch of his lips on her skin, and she could do nothing to endanger that feeling. She closed her mouth.

Matthew released her hand and settled back into his bench.

"No one has ever kissed my hand before," Sara murmured as she looked down at the back of her hand in bemusement. She looked up at him, embarrassed at her unplanned confession.

Matthew tilted his head, his smile almost shy. "Not even at the ball?"

Sara shook her head. "Not even at the ball. I've never been to a ball, not even a high school dance, frankly. My mother used to try to get me to go, buying me secondhand dresses to entice me, but no one ever asked, and I couldn't imagine going alone."

The words, spoken aloud, sounded pitiful, and Sara instantly regretted them.

Matthew seemed to think about her comment as if searching for the right response, and Sara didn't want to hear any sympathy.

"It's not important," she said dismissively, looking away toward the window. "I'm not sure why I mentioned it. Silly, really."

"It will be my pleasure to take you out onto the dance floor in the near future, Miss Reed."

Sara turned back, her heart rolling over. Matthew watched her steadily, and she melted under the gaze of his aquamarine eyes. How on earth could this Emily *not* want to marry him?

"Why thank you, Mr. Webster!" Sara replied with a shaky grin. Of course, there was *no* chance they would ever find themselves on a dance floor together in nineteen hundred or any other year, but the memory of his words would thrill her heart forever.

Never having had a boyfriend, Sara was unused to flirting. Her life had involved school, homework and a part-time job in a fast food joint when she got older. She had chosen to spend her free time with her mother who, because of her heart condition, could not work or even socialize. It hardly mattered though, as no boys had been particularly interested in her anyway.

Matthew, the handsome turn-of-the-century gentleman with impeccable manners and a courtly demeanor, presented a romantic figure beyond belief. If Sara hadn't been tossed into a cold jail cell, she might have thought Matthew was a figment of her imagination. She'd had an adolescent period of reading historical romance novels, but that habit had given way to high school homework and then college.

Matthew...the reality...surpassed every romantic character she'd ever read. The clean soapy scent of his clothing, the warmth of his hands, the tenderness of his lips and the strong beat of his heart when she pressed her hand on his chest all exceeded any expectations she might ever have had.

"For now though, perhaps we should get some sleep," he said. "Unless there is more you wish to disclose?" His smile teased.

Sara responded in kind, relieved that he was prepared to take a lighthearted approach for now to her evasive and mysterious answers.

"Nothing further," she intoned.

"Good night then. Sleep well, Sara," Matthew said. He turned off all lights except a small one near the compartment door before returning to his bench.

"Good night," Sara said. She kicked off her canvas shoes and fluffed the pillow on her own bench before reclining on her side and pulling the blanket up to her shoulders. She saw Matthew look down and study her shoes, but he said nothing.

He stuffed a pillow into a corner and settled himself, crossing his arms and stretching out his legs.

Sara fell asleep thinking that her first experience sleeping in the same room with a man was not quite what she had imagined. She smiled.

CHAPTER SEVENTEEN

In what seemed like only a few hours but was in reality about nine hours later, Matthew helped Sara down the steps of the train in Seattle. They had breakfasted early in the dining room, having decided that avoiding Mrs. Feeney was a moot point.

Sara's hand was cold in his, and she looked pale as she stared at the whirlwind of activity at the station. Horse-drawn carriages and wagons awaited passengers, luggage and goods. Some arrivals were greeted with embraces and cries of welcome, while others stood tiredly by, awaiting their bags.

"Is everything all right, Sara?" Matthew asked. "You look faint." He turned to face her.

"Yes, I'm fine," she whispered. "Just overwhelmed."

Matthew turned to survey the scene. "Yes, the Seattle train depot is busy, quite hectic at this time of day when the train arrives."

He tucked her hand under his arm.

"I need to get a porter and a carriage," he said. "Normally, my own carriage would await me, but I telegraphed to say that I had changed my plans and did not know when I would arrive."

He waylaid a porter and gave him directions. A familiar voice caught his ear.

"Matthew!"

Matthew whirled around, momentarily forgetting that he held Sara's hand under his arm.

Emily, lovely as always in a gray skirt and jacket, with a festive silk flowered hat that suited her fair coloring, waved as she hurried toward them. She slowed when she saw Sara.

Matthew drew in a sharp breath.

"Emily!" he said when she arrived at their side. "What brings you to the station?"

Emily, appraising Sara frankly with bright-blue eyes, turned to him with a questioning smile.

"But I always pick you up from your trips, Matthew. Your father sent word that you would arrive on the train today. Will you introduce me?"

She smiled at Sara, but Matthew knew Emily well enough to recognize that she was displeased. He had not yet formed a plan to explain Sara to his parents, much less to Emily or, in fact, any other acquaintances.

"Miss Sara Reed, this is Miss Emily Williams, a childhood friend."

Emily arched an eyebrow in his direction but held out her hand.

"Miss Reed, so nice to meet you."

"It's nice to meet you too," Sara said, taking Emily's hand in her own for a brief shake. Matthew felt Sara's grip on his arm tighten.

"Did you meet on the train?" Emily asked, directing her question to Matthew.

"Yes, we did. Miss Reed will be staying with us for a period of time." He thought he might as well take a bold stance.

"I beg your pardon?" Emily asked. Her brows narrowed as if in confusion.

"Miss Reed will be staying with us," he repeated, though he knew she had heard him the first time.

"Oh!" Emily said. Matthew wanted to confide in her, as he had always done, but Sara's secrets were not his to share, what secrets he knew. He felt her fingers biting into his arm, and he patted her hand reassuringly. Emily did not miss the gesture.

"Well, welcome to Seattle, Miss Reed. Is this your first visit?"

Sara nodded wordlessly.

The porter hurried up with Matthew's bag and the carpetbag Matthew had purchased for Sara's new clothing.

"Your father insisted I take your carriage, as he always does," Emily said. "It's just over there."

Matthew spotted Raymond, the driver, who had just settled the horses and was in the act of climbing down to assist the porter.

"That is most fortunate, Emily. I did not expect to see you here," he said, wishing the words unsaid as soon as he spoke them. "I am very grateful to both you and my father."

"Nonsense," Emily said. "Why wouldn't I be here?"

Matthew chose not to respond in front of Sara, for all he could say was that he thought Emily's rejection of his proposal meant they could no longer continue as friends.

"Thank you, Raymond," Matthew said as Raymond helped Sara and Emily into the closed carriage before loading Matthew's case.

Matthew took the seat across from Emily and Sara.

"Your father did not mention Miss Reed would be staying," Emily said with another arch of one eyebrow.

"He does not know," Matthew said evenly, careful to preserve a pleasant expression as Sara watched him.

"He will be most surprised, I think," Emily said.

"Yes," Matthew said. Despite his joy at seeing Emily, Matthew could not help but view her through a new light. Her comments at the moment seemed most inappropriate, given as they were in front of Sara as if she was not there.

"Pleasantly so, I am sure," Matthew added with a reassuring smile toward Sara.

"Of course," Emily added with a polite smile in Sara's direction. "Matthew's parents are delightful, very nice."

"Have you been well, Emily? Your family?" Matthew asked innocuously.

"Yes, thank you. Mother and father are well."

"Good," he said. At the moment, Matthew found it hard to think of polite conversation. His thoughts were on the hours ahead, as he must surely explain Sara's origins, of which he knew very little.

"And where are you from, Miss Reed?" Emily asked. Matthew held his breath to listen to Sara's answer, wondering if Emily had read his mind.

"Spokane," she said without elaborating. The carriage lurched forward, and Sara grabbed a strap. Matthew surmised she had never been in a carriage before, not surprising given her impoverished childhood circumstances.

She turned to stare out the window. Matthew caught Emily's eyes upon him. She quirked her eyebrow again as if to ask him a question, and he shook his head tiredly. He had not slept well the night before, concerning himself overly much with Sara and her future.

"How are my parents?" he asked.

"They were well. I had dinner with them last night and took the carriage from there so I could start early this morning."

"Thank you again for picking me up, Emily."

"I cannot think why I would not pick you up as I have always done," she murmured. Her cheeks tinged a rose color, and Matthew sighed inwardly. Emily had grown from a tomboy into a beautiful, poised young woman, one any man would be proud to call his wife.

Intelligent, educated and articulate, she graced many a dinner table with lively conversation. Though she had attended university with him, she had not pursued any sort of employment. Her family's wealth did not require that she do so. He had often wondered why she attended college, but she had a lively mind, and he had enjoyed their shared assignments and homework.

He pulled his gaze from her face and turned toward Sara. Sara watched him, her expression flat, without emotion. He smiled at her briefly, but she only lifted a corner of her mouth before turning away to look out the window.

She seemed somehow remote, distanced, and he wondered if it was due to their arrival in what was to her a strange city, or perhaps due to the uncertainty of her future.

"What do you think of Seattle, Miss Reed?" he asked, reverting to the formal use of her last name.

"It's big," she said. "Busy. Lots of horses and wagons."

"Well, of course," Emily said with a short laugh. Matthew directed a disapproving stare in her direction.

"Yes, it is a large city, larger than Spokane," Matthew said. "Given the hour, many people are on their way to work or making deliveries to businesses. The city settles down at night."

Sara nodded. "Yes, I'm sure it does." She turned a shoulder to Emily and returned to staring out of the carriage window.

Matthew had already deduced that these two women would not become friends, though he was not quite certain why. Sara seemed bent on ignoring Emily, and several of Emily's comments could be construed as less than civil.

He sighed heavily and followed Sara's gaze to stare out the window.

They arrived at his house on Queen Anne Hill in good time, and Raymond pulled the carriage up to the front door. He jumped down to open the carriage door, and Matthew climbed out to hand first Sara and then Emily down.

"You will stay for some coffee?" Matthew said. In the past, Emily had always stayed for coffee when she had picked him up at the station. They would discuss Matthew's most recent business trip and Emily's activities in his absence.

"Yes, thank you," Emily said. "Your father told me to say that he was expecting us."

On cue, his father appeared in the doorway, followed by his mother. A tall, slender man like his son, Harry Webster raised a hand in greeting. Susan Webster, petite like Sara, stood beside him, looking years younger than her actual age in a fetching lilac silk gown that she favored. His mother shared the same blonde hair as Emily and still kept her hair color, while his father's hair, chestnut like his own, had whitened over the years.

Emily moved to stand beside his parents.

"Matthew has brought a guest," she announced.

Matthew tucked Sara's hand under his arm and led her forward.

"Mother, Father, may I introduce Miss Sara Reed? Miss Reed, my father, Mr. Harry Webster, and my mother, Mrs. Susan Webster."

Impeccable manners prevented them from showing their surprise, as they must surely have been.

"Good to meet you, my dear," his father said jovially. "Come in. Let's have some coffee."

"Delightful to meet you, Miss Reed," his mother said. "Yes, please do come in. We usually have coffee together when Matthew returns from one of his trips so that he can regale us with tales of his travels."

His mother reached up to kiss Matthew on the cheek before taking Sara by the arm and turning toward the house. Emily tucked her hand into the crook of his father's arm, and Matthew found himself trailing the group into the house.

"Another cup of coffee for our guest, Mrs. Roe," Matthew's mother said as the housekeeper hurried up.

A plump woman of Irish descent who had been with his family for more years than Matthew could remember, Mrs. Roe accepted a quick embrace from him.

"Yes, ma'am," she said with a beam in Matthew's direction. She bustled off to the kitchen.

Matthew's mother led them across the large marble-tiled foyer and into the drawing room. Her favorite room in the house, she had decorated it in shades of green and rose, from the pale-green Oriental rug to the dark-rose sofas and forest-green easy chairs. Mahogany and cherrywood furnishings completed the room. A white marble fireplace dominated the center of the room, a warm fire crackling within. Rose-colored velvet curtains decorated the windows that looked out over the street in front of the house.

Matthew's mother led Sara to the one of the sofas and settled her there. Matthew took up a protective posture at the side of the sofa nearest Sara. His mother hesitated.

"Won't you sit, Matthew?" she asked. She seated herself next to Sara, and Matthew's father deposited Emily next to his wife before taking one of the easy chairs for himself.

"Yes, thank you. I will when the coffee comes, Mother."

"Welcome to our home, Miss Reed," his mother said. "I hope your journey was pleasant."

"Yes, thank you," Sara said.

Matthew watched as Sara characteristically laced and unlaced her fingers. She was nervous, and he could do little to ease her fears at the moment but stand beside her. He preferred to speak to his parents in private regarding Sara's stay, but the matter could not wait for Emily's departure.

"Miss Reed has come to stay with us for a period," Matthew said before any further conversation unfolded.

His father quirked an eyebrow, but a ready smile lightened his face.

"Wonderful!" he said. "So pleased to have you, my dear."

His mother, displaying an inordinate amount of restraint, smiled.

"We are so pleased to have you, Miss Reed."

"Thank you," Sara murmured. "I know this is unexpected."

"Not at all," Matthew's father said. "A lovely surprise."

Matthew breathed a sigh of relief. His parents had behaved as well as he might have hoped, and although he knew they would have questions for him in private, they were prepared to treat his guest civilly.

"Where do you call home, Miss Reed?" his mother asked.

"Spokane," she responded.

Mrs. Roe entered with a coffee service and set it on an oval mahogany table positioned between the sofas.

"I'll pour, thank you, Mrs. Roe," his mother said. "Miss Reed will be staying with us for a period of time, Mrs. Roe. Could you ask Lucy to make up a room for her?"

"Yes, ma'am," Mrs. Roe said. "Right away."

"Thank you."

Mrs. Roe left the room after a quick glance in Sara's direction.

"Coffee, Miss Reed?" Matthew's mother asked.

"Yes, please. Call me Sara."

"Of course. Thank you, Sara," his mother said. She poured coffee for everyone and settled back.

Matthew pulled one of the easy chairs toward the sofa and positioned himself at Sara's elbow. His mother noticed but said nothing.

"And what brings you to Seattle, Sara?" Matthew's father asked.

Sara threw a hasty look in Matthew's direction. He had not suggested a story they could agree on, because he did not want to lie to his parents. As he had told Sara earlier, lying was foreign to him.

"I met Sara in Kalispell, and she was traveling for pleasure. I convinced her of the beauty of the city, and she decided to see for herself."

That everyone in the room narrowed their eyes when they looked at him told Matthew that his fabrication had not been particularly successful. Even Sara regarded him with a dubious expression. However, his parents were too well mannered to question him further in the presence of others.

"It is quite beautiful here, my dear," his father said. "Quite beautiful. You will enjoy it."

"Yes," his mother agreed. "Seattle is beautiful, Sara, especially in the fall as the leaves change color."

"I have never been to Kalispell," Emily noted. "Did you have business there as well, Matthew?"

Matthew was not fooled by the innocent look on her face.

"Yes," he replied briefly. He could not imagine such a thing, but he wished Emily would leave so he could speak more freely with his parents. To wish Emily gone was contrary to all his sorrow over the past few weeks. And even beyond that, as she had been his lifelong confidant. He felt as if he hardly knew himself at the moment.

He looked away from Emily's face toward Sara, who watched him. She had been uncharacteristically silent since their arrival, and he could not blame her, but he missed the intimacy of their conversations. She regarded him now almost as if he were a stranger.

As if Emily could read his thoughts, she sighed, set her coffee cup down and rose.

"Well, I must go," she said. "Mother is having some friends over for lunch, and she would like for me to be there. I will send the carriage back. Matthew, could you walk me to the door?"

Matthew threw a quick glance in Sara's direction, then nodded.

"Yes, of course."

He followed her out of the drawing room, hoping that Sara would be comfortable with his parents.

As they neared the front door, Emily turned to him.

"I know you are not telling the truth about Miss Reed, Matthew, and I assume that you will explain everything to me in your own time. We have always shared our secrets. I need to know something now though. Should I consider Miss Reed a rival for your affections?"

Matthew's jaw slackened. Could he have heard right? His affections?

"I cannot pretend to understand what you are talking about, Emily," he said in exasperation. "Did you not soundly reject me only two weeks ago?"

Her cheeks colored, and she blinked.

"Well, that was then! I needed more time to think. I still need time to think."

Matthew's heart jumped for a moment, then settled into a dull thud in his chest.

"If you could have told me then that you need time to think about my proposal instead of summarily rejecting me, I would have been spared a great deal of misery."

Emily smiled brightly, her cheeks glowing.

"Oh, Matthew! Were you miserable? I am so sorry. I had just never thought of marrying you. I know our parents wished it, but I thought you felt the same way as I."

"The same way as you? Apparently not," Matthew said with a raised brow.

"That we were almost brother and sister," she said. "But I have reflected more, and I begin to think we could do well together."

"Do well together?" Matthew had thought the same thing at one time, but Emily's words chafed him now. They sounded sterile, denoting a life of convenience and comfort, but rarely interesting and hardly complex.

"Yes, isn't that what you want?"

Matthew thought of Sara, alone and trying to converse with his parents.

"I must return to the drawing room, Emily. You must do as you think best. If you wish to reconsider my proposal, then please do. I await your reply."

Emily's blue eyes widened, and her lips tightened with anger.

"If Miss Reed is more important to you than I am, Matthew, please do return to the drawing room! You can call on me when you are free. Good day!"

"Good day," Matthew said, equally angry. He held the door open for Emily, and she flounced out toward the waiting carriage.

CHAPTER EIGHTEEN

"I am so very sorry to hear about your mother, Sara," Mrs. Webster said. "You are an orphan then?"

Sara assumed that was Mrs. Webster's way of asking about her father. Since she was an adult, Sara hadn't really thought of herself as an orphan.

"Yes, I suppose I am."

"And you have no other family?"

Sara shook her head. "No." The conversation had taken on a depressingly sympathetic tone, and she wanted to change it.

"What a lovely room," she said, looking around.

Mrs. Webster smiled. "It is my favorite room in the house. I only allow my husband and son in here when we have guests. They have the library for their use."

"That is quite true, my dear," Mr. Webster said. "We are not allowed in here otherwise. A distinctly feminine room."

Sara had liked him instantly. Although Matthew's personality was probably more like his mother's, polite but a bit reserved, she saw occasional glints of his father's easygoing style. Certainly, Matthew shared his father's handsome looks and wide smile.

She sipped her coffee, wondering what else she could safely say that wouldn't arouse suspicion of her origins or elicit sympathetic glances for her "orphan" status.

Mrs. Webster was the picture of turn-of-the-century elegance in lavender satin and lace with an immaculate coif of still bright blonde hair. Mr. Webster, the image of what Matthew promised to be as an older man, matched his wife in style and grace. Unlike Matthew, he sported a broad, thick graying mustache, but his smile was as handsome as his

110

son's.

Matthew, however, was not smiling when he returned to the drawing room. His face was taut, his eyebrows drawn together in an expression of anger. She had only seen him that way on two occasions, and both were elicited by encounters with Mrs. Feeney. What had happened?

She would have to wait to ask Matthew, if she dared. It was likely something to do with Emily, and Sara wasn't sure she wanted to know, nor did she think Matthew would want to discuss it with her.

"Is everything all right, Matthew?" his mother asked.

"Yes, Mother, thank you." Matthew retook his seat and picked up his coffee. He turned to stare at the fire as if ignoring them, which surprised Sara. His manners were usually so perfect.

He drew in a long audible breath and turned back to his parents and Sara.

"Forgive me," he said. "I am certain you both have questions."

"Perhaps we should not trouble Sara with family matters, Matthew," his mother said, almost reprovingly.

"Nothing that cannot wait, son," his father agreed.

"If I may speak frankly, Sara would probably be more comfortable if she knew what I had to say rather than wondering what was said out of her presence."

"Oh, Matthew," his mother protested with an uncertain look in Sara's direction. His father straightened with an expression of interest.

Sara held her breath and waited to hear what Matthew had to say. She hoped he didn't mention her time in jail.

Matthew held up a hand. "If you do not object, Sara?"

Wordlessly, she shook her head.

"I was less than forthright when I said I met Sara in Kalispell. I actually met her on the train to Chicago. She had fallen on hard times. She left the train in Kalispell, and I found myself worrying about her welfare. On my return trip to Seattle, I found her in Kalispell and discovered that her situation had worsened to such an untenable degree that she was in jeopardy. She is without family or friends. I convinced her to return to Seattle with me."

Sara set her coffee down on the side table. Matthew's version of events raised more questions than provided answers.

"I realize how mysterious that all sounds, and I promise I won't trouble you for long," she said to his parents. "I really won't."

"You won't be any trouble at all, my dear. Any friend of Matthew's is a friend of ours," his father said with a broad smile.

"Yes, of course, Sara," his mother replied. "We are only too happy to help. Matthew, I hope that Emily reminded you we are committed to the

Williamses' get-together tomorrow night for a small dinner and dance. I know they would love to have Sara as well. I will send them a note in the morning."

"Oh, wait..." Sara began. "I don't think—"

"Nonsense, my dear. Of course you must come. We cannot leave you here languishing in your room alone. It will be a good opportunity to introduce you to folks," Mr. Webster said. He looked down at his pocket watch. "Now, if you will excuse me, I have some correspondence to attend to before lunch." He rose, and Mrs. Webster rose when he did.

"I need to check with Sally about lunch," she said. "I'll see you to your room first, Sara."

"Mrs. Roe and I can accompany Sara to her room, Mother. Go see about lunch."

Mrs. Webster nodded.

"Yes, that will be fine." They left the room, and Sara let out the breath she felt like she'd been holding since her arrival.

"That was awkward, but I don't imagine there was any other way to handle it," she said.

Matthew stood and held out a hand to help her rise from the couch.

"Yes, I know. I apologize most sincerely for embarrassing you."

"Well, you didn't embarrass me more than I've embarrassed myself, that's for sure. I really do appreciate all you're doing for me, Matthew. Your parents are great!"

"They are wonderful, aren't they? My mother surprised me. I thought she might have more questions. Perhaps she does, and I have not yet heard them."

"They're very kind to take a stranger in."

"Oddly, I do not feel as if you are a stranger, Sara."

She smiled and asked the question uppermost in her mind.

"If you don't mind my asking, did you and Emily have a fight?"

Matthew, on the point of guiding Sara from the room with a hand to her back, paused and turned toward her.

He nodded.

"I would not normally discuss such a matter, but over the past few days, given the unusual nature of our friendship, I feel we have achieved a certain familiarity, which allows me to confide in you."

Sara nodded. She hadn't been entirely honest with him, but he was aware of that and accepted it for now.

"It seems as if Emily has rethought my marriage proposal and is now willing to consider it."

Sara's heart dropped to somewhere far, far below her stomach.

"I knew it!" she muttered. "I *knew* she would. I couldn't believe she would turn you down."

Matthew blinked and reared his head at the vehemence of her words.

"I think I must take that as a compliment, Sara. Thank you! I have never known Emily to waver in any of her decisions. She thinks we would 'do well together.'"

"Do well together?" Sara repeated. "What does *that* mean?" She understood the words, but she wondered what Emily meant specifically.

Matthew shrugged. "I suppose she means that we suit one another, since we have known each other most of our lives and share a common background."

"Oh!" Sara said, inwardly wincing at the dull and uninteresting vision of Matthew's future. He deserved so much more. He deserved a woman who loved him absolutely and completely, a woman who loved him with passion, not one who "suited" him.

"Congratulations," she murmured, swallowing hard. "When do you plan on getting married?"

Matthew grimaced. "Emily has not yet made up her mind. I cannot very well withdraw the proposal, even if I wanted to."

Sara's head shot up.

"*Do* you want to?"

"I am not certain. Before now, I had never envisioned a future in which Emily was not my wife. However, the past few weeks gave me time to reflect, albeit at times morosely and piteously, as I mourned the loss of what I thought I desired."

"So, what are you going to do?"

"I must await Emily's decision."

Sara wanted to influence him. She wanted to tell him that he shouldn't have to wait for Emily to make up her mind. The woman had made it up once before, and she had turned him down. Ignore her change of heart! Take back the proposal! Forget about her!

But Sara pressed her lips together and kept her mouth shut. It wasn't her place to interfere in Matthew's life, and certainly not in the life of someone from another time.

"I do not suppose you have any words of wisdom to offer me?" Matthew asked with a small chuckle.

Sara shook her head. "I do, but I'll keep them to myself. I'm not sure they're particularly wise. I've never been in love, and I'm hardly an expert on matters of the heart." Sara bit her tongue. Why on earth had she added the last sentence?

Matthew cocked his head and studied her face. Her cheeks heated, and she blinked.

"Still, I would be interested to hear your thoughts at some point, Sara.

I wonder now if I have ever been in love before myself."

Before Sara could reply, Mrs. Roe entered the room and announced that Sara's room was ready. They escorted Sara up a curving, carpet-covered marble staircase to the second floor, and Mrs. Roe showed Sara to her room.

The bedroom clearly reflected Mrs. Webster's touch—a palette of soft blue and rose with dark mahogany furniture. A huge four-poster bed with a satin rose coverlet dominated the room. Blue velvet curtains matched the blue brocade on several easy chairs set before a small marble fireplace. A dressing table and standing oval mirror hugged one wall next to a wardrobe. Her carpetbag rested in front of the wardrobe.

On arrival, her quick survey of the exquisitely graceful exterior of the large Queen Anne-style house had hinted at a luxurious interior, and that had proven true. The Websters seemed to have a lot of money.

"Lunch will be ready at half past twelve as usual, Mister Matthew," Mrs. Roe said. "If there's nothing else?"

"No, thank you, Mrs. Roe," he said.

She turned away, and Matthew pointed to a connecting door. "There is a bathroom through there." He looked down at his pocket watch. "I hope you are hungry. Sally is the best cook in Seattle, in my opinion. Lunch will be served in a little over an hour. Hopefully, that will give you time to attend to your needs."

Was it already 11:30? It seemed as if the train had just arrived.

"Thank you," she said.

He eyed her for a moment.

"Is everything all right, Sara? I know you must feel very lost right now, given that you are in a strange city and a strange house, but you can always confide in me."

"I'm fine," she said with a nod. Matthew would never know how lost she felt at the moment. She had no idea how she'd traveled in time or why, and no idea how to get back. Looking at his handsome face, she had no idea what she would even go back to.

He hesitated as if choosing his next words carefully.

"Please do not disappear, Sara. It would be unsafe for you to vanish into a large city like Seattle, and not only would it distress my parents, it would distress me. Additionally, I believe you owe me a dance."

CHAPTER NINETEEN

Following lunch, Matthew offered to take Sara on a drive through the city.

"Oh, yes!" she breathed.

"What a wonderful idea, Matthew!" his mother said. "I am sure Sara will enjoy that."

"I still have some correspondence to finish. Enjoy yourselves," his father said with a broad smile as he left the dining room.

"Very well," Matthew said with an equally broad smile. "I will wait by the front door while you go get your shawl and a hat."

Matthew's mother lingered in the dining room after Sara left in search of her outer garments. As Matthew stood to leave, his mother detained him with a hand on his arm.

"Matthew, dear, what are your plans for Sara? And I do not mean a drive around the city this afternoon. What do you propose to do with her?" She shook her head. "I do not like that wording, but I cannot think how else to ask the question."

Matthew sighed heavily.

"I am not certain, Mother. I did not have time to tell you before I left, or perhaps I was too glum to do so, but I asked Emily to marry me the day before I left for Chicago."

"Matthew!" His mother's joyous smile made him wince. "Oh, Matthew! How wonderful! Of course she accepted!"

Matthew shook his head. "No, she did not." His mother's face fell, and he hastened to clarify the matter. "Emily stated she considered me a brother but not a potential husband. And I grieved during the weeks that I was gone. But upon my return yesterday, Emily said she wished to reconsider her rejection of my proposal, that she felt we would do well together."

His mother stared at him, no doubt attempting to absorb all that he had said. Myriad emotions showed in her expressions, from elation to confusion to anger. Her next words surprised him.

"Do well together? What could she possibly mean by that?" Her blue eyes glittered and narrowed. "A marriage is not a business arrangement, at least no marriage that my son will enter." Her chin firmed. "Is she saying that she does not love you? I always imagined that the two of you would marry."

"I did as well, Mother," he said on a sigh. "I imagine Emily means that since we know each other well, we would get along well."

"But I do not want you to marry just to *get along*," she said. "I want you to marry for love!"

Matthew's face reddened. Her words reminded him of Sara's words.

"I did not realize you were such a romantic, Mother. I would like to marry for love as well. I thought I loved Emily. Perhaps I do, and I am simply angry with her for her initial rejection."

"Well, *I* am angry, too," she said. "Not that Emily might not wish to marry you, but that she thinks you should 'do well together.'"

Matthew regarded his mother with surprise. She rarely expressed anger.

"And what about Sara?" she asked. "My original question was about her future, but somehow I feel her future must be tied into the question of whether you will proceed with a marriage to Emily."

He heard Sara descend the stairs, and he placed a hasty kiss on his mother's cheek.

"I cannot say for now, Mother," he said. "I must go."

Moments later, he handed Sara up into the carriage, and they set off for a delightful tour of the city. Matthew, having lived in Seattle all of his life, enjoyed seeing it through Sara's fresh, if cryptically unusual, perspective.

"Tall ships!" she sighed. "Real tall ships." They had stopped near the pier at Elliot Bay at her request, although he felt the area a little rough for a lady.

"Yes," he said. "Tall ships. I take it you have not seen such ships before?"

"Only in the movies," she said. She cast a hasty glance at him and pressed her lips together.

"Moovees?"

"It's a Spokane thing," she murmured. "You probably haven't heard of them."

Matthew opened his mouth to ask for clarification, but Sara's face had taken on that shuttered look that had come to distress him. He chose to leave the subject alone.

They had moved on to tour the downtown area, where Sara asked if they might ride a streetcar.

"I've never been on a trolley," she said with glee as they boarded the streetcar. Matthew directed Raymond to pick them up several miles further up Second Avenue. Never a fan of public transportation, he did his best to tolerate Sara's enthusiasm for the thankfully short journey.

"Come now, Sara. I am certain they have streetcars in Spokane. I have seen them."

"Really?" she asked as she glanced at him before returning her attention to the bustling activity on Second Avenue. She had found a seat on an exterior bench, which required that Matthew stand at her side and hang on to a pole. A glance at the interior of the crowded car convinced him that he was in the best position possible.

"Are you saying you are not aware Spokane has streetcars? How is that possible?"

She shrugged but avoided looking at him. "Too poor, I guess."

Matthew frowned at her short answer. Certainly, he firmly believed that she had grown up impoverished, but to have never had enough money even to board a streetcar seemed very poor indeed.

To Matthew's relief, the short ride ended, and they proceeded on to a tea room to have an afternoon refreshment.

Upon entering the restaurant, Sara pulled the pin from her hat and dragged it from her head.

"Uh oh," she said as they followed a waitress to the table. "I'm supposed to keep my hat on, aren't I?"

Matthew, who had removed his derby and overcoat, followed her gaze around the room. He had given the matter little thought, but yes, it did seem as if all the women continued to wear their hats inside.

"Let me hazard a guess. You do not wear hats in Spokane, either?"

Sara, trying to reposition her hat without success, grimaced. "That would be a 'too poor' answer?"

"You phrase that as a question. Are you asking me?" His lips twitched. Sara was both mystifying and intriguing, and he found himself increasingly captivated by the combination.

Sara sighed and pulled her hat from her head to set it on the seat beside her.

"No, not really. Too poor," she said without meeting his gaze. She picked up the menu and surveyed it, her eyes widening.

"Nice prices!" she said.

"Please do not tell me you have never been in a tea room before.

Surely you must have."

Sara looked up from the menu. "Tea room? No, I don't think I have," she said. The corner of her mouth lifted as if she repressed a smile. Matthew felt she must have been teasing him. "I've been to a coffee shop, if that helps."

"A coffee shop sounds very similar to a tea room," he said. "Perhaps coffee is more prevalent in Spokane than in Seattle."

"Oh, I seriously doubt that," Sara said with a wide grin.

Matthew cocked his head, as if in doing so, he could understand her enigmatic remarks better.

"I predict that Seattle will become a paradise for coffee lovers," she said.

"Why do you say that? I admit that I prefer coffee, and they do have coffee here in the tea room, but it is not particularly good. Tea is their specialty."

"I'm just guessing," she said. "Just guessing."

The waitress returned, and they placed their order. Matthew watched Sara as she surveyed the room.

"I could probably get a job at a place like this," she said. "If I were going to stay in Seattle."

He drew in a sharp breath. "In a tea room? Oh, no! Certainly not!" he said.

She drew her brows together into a severe expression.

"Don't be a snob, Matthew. I'll need to get a job somewhere. I don't know what jobs there are for woman in the twentieth—in Seattle. I can't live off your parents forever, and I suspect you'll be marrying and moving on soon, won't you?"

Matthew stared at her. She had raised three issues in one short barrage of words, and one caught his attention more than the others.

Her reference to "twentieth." Did she mean the "twentieth century?" An odd phrase. Even now that it was the fall of nineteen hundred, he was still unused to calling the new millennium the twentieth century. He had lived the majority of his life in the nineteenth century.

"You said you did not know what jobs were available for women in the twentieth century. I must say that strikes me as an odd turn of phrase."

Sara dropped her gaze to the white linen tablecloth and waved her hand dismissively. "More importantly, I can't stay with your parents forever, not once you're married. Emily will come to live at your house, won't she?"

Matthew had the impression that she prevaricated.

"I do not think I ever asked you, Sara. Did you hold a job in Spokane?

What did you do?"

"I worked in the school cafeteria. That's how I know I could work in a tea room."

"What school?"

She shook her head. "That hardly matters. What about you?"

"What school, Sara? Please humor me."

"I told you there are things I can't explain," she said, her eyes darting about as if she were trapped.

"Surely you can tell me what school you attended, Sara. Such an innocuous question." Against his better judgment, Matthew continued his dogged inquisition.

"Gonzaga! Okay? Gonzaga! It's just a school!"

Matthew blinked. "Gonzaga? But Gonzaga is only for men."

Sara drew in a sharp breath.

"Really? I should have known," she muttered. She held her hands up in a helpless gesture. "I've got nothing."

Matthew leaned forward.

"I understand you are withholding information from me, Sara, but please do not lie to me."

"Then don't ask me questions," she murmured, her eyes downcast. "And for the record, I do go to Gonzaga, men's college or not."

Matthew knew a deep sense of shame. He should not have pressed Sara such that she lied to him. It was unlikely that a young woman from such an impoverished background could afford to attend Gonzaga University, nor did it accept women. But why did she feel the need to lie?

"Please forgive me for hounding you with questions, Sara, especially when I said I would not. You are such a mystery to me that I occasionally weaken and want to know more. I trust you will tell me everything in time, but I can see you are not yet ready."

Sara shook her head.

"As for employment," Matthew said. "Please delay any action on that. If you must take employment in the future, I would prefer you work for my family's company. We have a few lady clerks who seem to be quite happy."

Sara sighed heavily, and Matthew had the distinct impression he had said something that saddened or displeased her. The clerk positions in their business were highly sought after and prestigious jobs, and he did not understand the source of her displeasure.

"These positions do not appeal to you?"

She shook her head. "Oh, no, that sounds wonderful. Thank you." Her tone belied her words.

"As for the question of Emily, I do not know what the future holds, but no, if I were to marry Emily, I would not bring her to my parents' home. I would establish my own residence. However, that prospect is not only far distant but not a certainty."

"When will you decide?"

"It is no longer my decision, but Emily's. I must stand by my proposal if she wishes to reconsider it. I am certain that is what I wish, and as I told my mother, I think I must still be angry with her for her initial rejection. That is the only thing which could explain my unexpected lack of enthusiasm at her reversal."

"Yes, that must be it," Sara said quietly.

Matthew regarded her. Lustrous brunette hair, swept on top of her head, dropped to curls at the nape of her neck and nestled in the lace of her high-necked shirtwaist. Her skin, as pale as the ivory in her blouse, enticed one to run gentle fingers along her cheekbones. Her mouth, wide and beautiful when smiling, had settled into a frown.

"Yes, that must be it," he echoed.

CHAPTER TWENTY

"I think I will not go into the office today," Matthew announced the next morning at breakfast. "I must sign some documents tomorrow, which my secretary tells me are vital, but other than that, I believe I will take a few days off."

Sara tried to hide her smile of delight.

"The office will run without you, son. That is the benefit of having well-trained assistants," his father said with a knowing nod.

"Yes, exactly," Matthew agreed. He smiled broadly in Sara's direction, and her heart fluttered. After the tense conversation they'd had yesterday, she knew the time had come to tell him about herself, but she dreaded the moment. It was likely he wouldn't favor her with his winsome grin once he heard her babble about time travel and such.

"That is an excellent plan, Matthew," his mother said, delicately patting at her mouth with a linen napkin. "I am certain Sara will be most pleased." She smiled at Sara.

Matthew's aquamarine eyes twinkled when he looked at Sara, and a thrill ran up her spine.

The door to the dining room opened, and Emily stepped into the room.

"Good morning, dear ones," she said.

"Good morning, Emily!" Mr. Webster exclaimed. "Welcome, as always, my dear. Have you come to join us for breakfast?"

"Yes, I thought I might before I attend to some errands for mother for the dinner and dance tonight."

"Good morning, Emily," Mrs. Webster said.

"Good morning, Matthew, Miss Reed." She nodded in Sara's direction, her smile polite, though not quite reaching her eyes.

Matthew rose to pull out a chair, and Emily beamed at him as she took a seat.

Sara knew then that Emily was reconsidering Matthew's proposal because of *her*, because Matthew had brought her home. It seemed likely that Emily had taken her childhood friend, Matthew, for granted, but the arrival of a strange woman in the mix had stirred things up.

"Thank you, Matthew," Emily said. "I was wondering if you could help me with a few of my errands this morning, Matthew. There is still so much to do for the dinner, and I really do not feel as if I can do everything."

Matthew hesitated for a moment, his eyes flying to Sara's face. Sara looked away.

"I committed myself to entertaining Miss Reed today, Emily, but if she is willing and you do not mind, I am certain we can both be of assistance to you," he said.

Sara brought her napkin to her mouth to hide her gasp. No!

Emily opened and shut her mouth. She nodded. "Yes, that would be lovely," she said.

"What an excellent solution," Mrs. Webster said. "Just help yourself to the sideboard, Emily. You know we are informal for breakfast."

Emily shook her head. "I think that I am not really hungry after all," she said. "I will just have some coffee." She poured herself a cup of coffee from a nearby carafe.

"Are you enjoying your stay in Seattle, Miss Reed?" Emily asked.

"Sara, please." Sara nodded. "Yes, I am, thank you." At the moment, Sara was brainstorming a number of ways to get out of this "run around and do errands with Emily and Matthew" thing.

"I did not hear yesterday," Emily said. "How long will you be staying in Seattle?"

"That has not yet been determined," Matthew said.

"Oh, I see," Emily said. She toyed with her coffee and turned to speak to Mr. and Mrs. Webster about the dinner and dance that evening.

Sara glanced at Matthew, who seemed to study Emily's profile with a frown on his face. She had no way of knowing what he was thinking. He had set himself up as her protector almost from the first moment she had met him on the train, and he continued in that vein, even to the point of answering for her when questions became difficult. Although she had never had a man involve himself in her life as thoroughly as Matthew did, she didn't particularly dislike the sensation. At the moment, she needed his help to navigate the early twentieth century.

But his championing of her, his instinct to protect her as one would a stray puppy, would put a strain on his relationship with Emily. Sara couldn't help but feel glad of it, but she was also ashamed of her pettiness. Emily and Matthew had known each other for a long time. They really were more suited to each other and would "do well together," though Sara hated the term. Maybe the secret to a long and successful union in the nineteen hundreds *was* compatibility and not the passion that she felt for Matthew.

Sara realized that somehow, over the course of the past few weeks, she had fallen in love with Matthew—completely and irrevocably. She had fallen in time and fallen in love. Could she have found a man like Matthew in the twenty-first century? It was unlikely. Had time, finding her the perfect man, albeit in another century, made a course correction and brought her to meet him?

Or was this all some crazy dream that she would soon awaken from, to find herself in her apartment in Spokane, her head slumped on her desk? If so, she certainly had a vivid imagination.

She looked up and caught Matthew watching her, his head cocked in that inquisitive way he had, a gentle smile on his face. She lifted her lips and nodded, almost as if to tell him how she felt.

His smile gave way to a handsome broad grin, and he pressed his napkin to his mouth and rose.

"Are you ready, Emily? Sara?"

"Sara will need to get her outdoor things," his mother said. Sara welcomed the reminder. The house was warm, making it easy to forget how chilly it probably was outside. Further, Sara wasn't sure she was ever going to remember to grab a hat unless someone reminded her.

She skedaddled up the stairs, still wishing she could get out of the little errand adventure coming up. In fact, she wasn't looking forward to the dinner and dance either. She had no idea what to wear or how she was going to talk to still more people from another century.

Emily really only had a few errands and none that she needed Matthew for. As Sara had suspected, it had only been a ploy to get him to herself, and Sara wondered why Matthew had insisted she come along. She could have easily entertained herself with a walk around the Queen Anne Hill neighborhood. Even in Spokane, she had heard of the luxurious mansions on Seattle's Queen Anne Hill.

They rode in Emily's carriage, stopping by a flower shop to confirm that flowers were being delivered. Emily ordered a few more, consulting with Matthew as she did so, but Sara suspected Emily did so only to justify asking Matthew to come along.

Emily then directed her driver to a large brownstone near the center of Seattle. The city was large, even in nineteen hundred, and Sara felt thoroughly lost and disoriented. Horse-drawn wagons in every configuration gave the street facing the brownstone a congested and noisy atmosphere.

"Mother forgot to send an invitation to Mr. and Mrs. Greenwood, and they insist on having a formal invitation before they will attend, so I must drop it off. I will only be a moment."

Matthew stepped down to hand Emily from the carriage, and he stood by the carriage door while she walked up the sidewalk to the front door.

"Matthew," Sara hissed from inside the carriage. "Why on earth did you drag me out with you guys? It's obvious Emily wanted to talk to you alone."

Matthew turned and looked up into Sara's face. His blue eyes seemed to look directly into her soul, and she struggled for air.

"I could not abandon you," he said simply.

"I would have been fine on my own. I would have taken a walk or something," Sara added.

"No, no, you cannot walk unattended, Sara," he said with a shake of his head.

"Oh, please, Matthew! In your quiet neighborhood? Nothing is going to happen to me there. It's not like I'm walking around here in downtown Seattle. I would be lost down here. I already am!"

He opened his mouth to speak and then pressed his lips together.

"What aren't you saying, Matthew?" Sara asked.

Matthew seemed to swallow hard.

"I worry that you will disappear, Sara," he said.

Sara looked down into his sincere eyes, a shadow of concern dulling their brightness.

"Oh, Matthew," she sighed, allowing her face to show the love she felt. For all she knew, she might disappear the next day, thrown back into her own time. There were no guarantees.

"Why do you worry about me so much?" she asked quietly.

"I do not know," he said, "but I do. There is something about you that compels me to worry, to protect you, to look after you as a father might a child. There is a naïveté about you that seems particularly poignant."

"As a father might a child?" she choked out.

He blinked. "Did I say something to offend you?"

"So, you feel paternally toward me?"

"Yes?"

"Are you asking me or telling me?" Sara said.

"I am trying to give you the answer you want," he stated with a lift of one eyebrow.

"Well, I would have *much* preferred knight in shining armor and a damsel in distress," she sputtered. "I wouldn't know what to do with a father."

Matthew looked over his shoulder. Emily had stepped inside for a moment. He leaned into the carriage and took one of her hands in his.

"You are angry, Sara. What have I said? Do you wish me to be your knight in shining armor?"

"Well, that would be a darn sight better than my father. I really don't see you as my father," she muttered. Against her will, she gripped his hand. He responded.

"Then a knight in shining armor it shall be," he said with a grin. "But with the caveat that someday soon, you must tell me of your distress, fair damsel, else I will not know how to help you."

He pressed her hand to his lips, and her heart thudded. Over his shoulder, she saw Emily returning, and she pulled her hand from his.

"I think you should drop me off and take a drive with Emily," Sara said, though that was the last thing she wanted, ever.

"Yes, I think you must be right, Sara," he said with a sigh. "Will you be there when I return?"

"I will be there," Sara said.

They dropped her off in front of Matthew's house, and Matthew went on with Emily. Sara didn't go straight into the house but watched the carriage drive away.

Matthew had made it clear that if Emily wanted to proceed with the engagement, he was committed to following through. Within the next few hours, on Matthew's return, Sara would know if the engagement was on.

She wished at the moment that she could disappear. She turned and looked toward the house. If she went inside, Mrs. Webster would probably ask questions about Matthew's whereabouts, and Sara didn't feel up to answering them. She decided on a walk.

She pulled her shawl more tightly around her shoulders and headed away from the house, momentarily expecting someone to call out to her. When no one did, she relaxed and took in the sights as she walked. The view of the bay was spectacular, bustling with the tall ships she had seen the day before, and with steam ships, schooners and little boats she couldn't even name.

Queen Anne Hill wasn't as thickly developed as she had imagined it would be, given its famous name. Instead of numerous mansions fronting tree-lined and well-paved roads with concrete sidewalks, the unpaved dirt road she followed held only one or two of the immense and decorative houses per block. The landscape was barren of the green trees she thought Seattle was known for, no doubt timbered for both fuel and construction. Sadly, the deforestation was what allowed her to see the bay.

When the road curved to the right, Sara followed it to the end, where it then curved to the left as it resumed its downward descent. She hoped she wasn't getting herself lost. She turned to look back up the hill to spot the Webster house but couldn't see it. She shrugged, promising herself that she would retrace her steps, and she resumed her trek.

At some point, Sara noted that the hem of her skirts had absorbed a great deal of the loose dirt that passed for a road. With a frown, she lifted her skirts, wondering if she should turn back. Maybe a walk hadn't been such a good idea. The Queen Anne neighborhood felt a little more rugged and remote than she had imagined when she saw it from the carriage.

Still, what would she do at the house? Stare at the walls and wait for Matthew to return with news she didn't want to hear? Have tea with Mrs. Webster and dance around questions about her origins? None of those appealed to her.

Sara walked on, heading down the hill, admiring the broad vista of the bay. Suddenly, a searing pain shot through her foot as she stepped into a rut. With a cry, she fell forward into the road. She rolled to her side to grab her burning ankle through the mass of skirts. She must have twisted it—at least, that's all she hoped she had done. The pain was overwhelming.

Cursing and fighting back tears, Sara struggled to sit up, nursing her ankle as she did so. Dirt embedded itself in her blouse and skirt. Her hat had fallen off, and her shawl lay on the ground. She tried to push herself to a standing position, but caught by her skirt and petticoats, she fell over again.

She looked up at her unfamiliar surroundings. The nearest house was a block away, too far for her even to shout. The hill now seemed more isolated than ever. No pedestrians walked the roads, no carriages rolled by.

A sudden sense of panic overtook her, robbing her of air. How was she supposed to get back? She didn't really even know where she was. Pain and shortness of breath made her dizzy, but she tried to push herself up again. She couldn't just sit in the road. Her ankle had begun to throb unbearably.

The sound of rumbling wheels and jingling of a harness caught her attention. A carriage! Matthew? She twisted at the waist and looked behind her.

The carriage slowed, then stopped. A face peered out of the window, but it wasn't Matthew.

"Miss! Are you injured?" the man asked. The carriage door flew open, and a tall, slender man jumped down.

"Hold the horses, John," he said as he moved to her side. Well dressed, he wore a black derby and dark-gray overcoat. A thick gray mustache covered his mouth.

He came down on one knee in front of her. She noted irrelevantly that his shoes were immaculately shined.

"I think I twisted my ankle," she said, panting with pain. "I was out walking."

He looked down at the ankle she held but did not attempt to touch her.

"We must get you to a doctor. Do you have a physician?" His voice held a pleasant rumble.

Sara's mother had taught her never to accept rides from strangers, and since they couldn't afford a car, Sara had been offered rides more than she cared to remember. But through all four seasons of every year, she had marched doggedly on through the streets of Spokane, to school, to her part-time job, and home.

"If you could just drop me at the Webster house?" she said hoarsely. "Do you know where that is?"

He shook his head. "No, I am afraid I do not know that house. I was just visiting someone on business. Is the Webster house on this street?" He turned and scanned the houses.

"No, it's further up the hill," she said. The throbbing in her ankle intensified. "I'm not sure what street it's on. I've been walking for a while."

"I cannot believe you were out walking alone," he said. "We can either search for your house, or I can take you to my physician. I think the latter is the wisest course."

Sara had no idea how she was supposed to pay for a doctor. She thought the first idea was best.

"Do you mind trying to find the house? I'm staying with the Websters, and I really don't have any way to pay for a doctor."

"I am certainly willing to try, but please do not worry about the doctor's fees. That can all be taken care of. Can you stand?"

"I've been trying, but I keep falling over these skirts," she said.

"Let me help," he said. He held out his hands, and Sara slipped hers into his. Soft and gentle—she assumed he didn't do manual labor. He pulled, and she tried to push herself to a standing position, but another searing pain shot through her ankle, and she cried out.

"Wait! Wait!" she said breathlessly.

"Oh, my poor girl," he said. "Come, let me lift you." He ran his arm around her back and pulled her up to her feet...or to one foot. Sara balanced on the injured foot.

He supported her while she hopped over to the carriage. With a great deal of awkwardness, he half pushed her into the carriage, and she slumped against the seat, fighting a wave of dizziness.

"Let me get your hat and shawl," he said. He retrieved her things and disappeared from sight. Sara heard him talking to the driver but couldn't make out the words. He climbed in, laid her things on the bench beside her and sat down on the opposite bench.

With her leg down, the pulsating pain intensified, and Sara felt as if she was on the verge of passing out. She licked her dry lips.

"My name is Joseph Conrad," he said.

"I feel awful," she whispered. The coach moved forward, and darkness descended.

CHAPTER TWENTY-ONE

Matthew alighted from the carriage and waved to Emily's driver. They had deposited Emily at her house, and the driver had returned Matthew to his.

He entered the house and paused to listen for the sound of voices. He heard his father and mother in the drawing room, no doubt having tea, given the hour.

He drew in a deep breath, both anxious to see Sara and dreading it. He had a feeling she would be able to read his face.

Driving down by Lake Union, he and Emily had talked at length without the rancor that had accompanied their conversation yesterday.

"Have you made a decision yet, Emily?" he had asked without preamble.

"I did," she replied. "I would be pleased to marry you, Matthew. I apologize for my initial rejection. The question came as such a surprise to me."

Matthew's heart dropped, but he masked his face.

"I am so pleased," he said. "You were right. We should do well together."

"Yes, I think so," she said with a smile. "You and I have known each other far too long to imagine ourselves in love now. I love you. I am certain of it. Having known you so long, how could I not?"

"How could you not?" he echoed.

"And I think that you love me. You did ask me to marry you."

Matthew nodded. "Yes, I did."

"Then there is no reason we should not marry."

"None," Matthew agreed. His thoughts were elsewhere though, on the moment when he would tell Sara that he was in fact going to marry

Emily after all.

"Will you tell Miss Reed that we are to be married?"

Matthew, still lost in thought, blinked. "Miss Reed? Why would you ask that?"

Emily shrugged. "Well, she will have to find other arrangements, won't she?"

Matthew cocked his head.

"Because I am affianced? Why should that affect her?"

"Well, it isn't quite proper for her to stay at your house if you are engaged, Matthew."

Matthew stared at Emily.

"I do not intend to throw her from the house," he said firmly.

"But people will talk, Matthew. You know how they are."

"I do not care," he said. "Let them talk."

"I do not want to be the subject of gossip, Matthew!"

"I understand that, Emily. Neither do I, but I hardly think that having a guest staying in my home, in my mother's and father's home, would be a source for gossip."

"I believe Mrs. Feeney would disagree with you."

Matthew blinked. "Mrs. Feeney?"

"Yes, Matthew, Mrs. Feeney. You probably did not know, but she is a childhood friend of my mother's. She came to the house yesterday for tea and told us some outlandish story concerning a woman from Spokane who stole her clothing from a train station in Kalispell, Montana, and who was arrested and jailed for such."

Matthew drew in a sharp breath.

"I said nothing, but I suspected that was Miss Reed. Mrs. Feeney noted that a gentleman from Seattle, a Mr. Matthew Webster, had made reparations on the woman's behalf. You! Why would you do such thing? Why would you involve yourself in the crime of a strange woman?"

"You do not understand the entirety of the matter, Emily," he said harshly.

"Then enlighten me. We used to tell each other everything! Tell me why you would do such a thing?"

"I cannot explain it. She needed help," he said simply.

"But she is a criminal!" Emily cried.

"Emily, please. Do not speak of Miss Reed in that way. I will not stand for it! There are things that you do not understand."

"Then explain them to me, Matthew! Explain them to me!"

"I cannot!"

Emily's red cheeks paled, and she stared at him.

"Are you choosing Miss Reed over me, Matthew?" she whispered.

"No, of course not," he ground out. "Do not be silly. Do not concern yourself with her or with Mrs. Feeney's gossip."

"But Mrs. Feeney is coming tonight, Matthew. Mr. and Mrs. Feeney are coming to the dinner and dance tonight."

Matthew drew in a sharp breath and shook his head.

"Then I am afraid it would not be in Miss Reed's best interests to attend," he said flatly.

"No, I do not think she should," Emily said.

"And I shall not attend either."

"Matthew!" Emily remonstrated. "Of course you must attend! Do you not want to announce our engagement? Miss Reed is fully capable of staying home alone. That is, if you do not worry about your silver."

At her words, Matthew leaned out and rapped on the carriage door. "Please take Miss Williams home, Samuel!" he barked. He pulled his head back in and glared at Emily.

"I do not wish to announce our engagement tonight, Emily, and I will not be able to attend. You and I both have some thinking to do about whether we should 'do well together.' I understand that you are concerned about gossip, about Mrs. Feeney, but your comments are uncharitable. Sara is in my care. She is under my protection, and I will not have you disparage her further."

Emily's eyes flashed, and she crossed her arms over her stomach.

"So, it is *Sara* now, is it? Yes, you are right, Matthew. We do have some thinking to do. I do not think I even know you right now, and I have no idea what hold this woman has over you. You behave as if you are besotted with her, but that seems unlikely, given that you only recently met her. Do not take your charge of knight in shining armor too seriously, Matthew. I know you, and I am willing to marry you as you are. I am not, however, willing to marry a man who picks up strays and brings them home."

Now, only a short while later, Matthew rested his hand on the drawing room door. He had no idea whether he was engaged to be married or not. And the news that Mrs. Feeney continued to spread gossip was disturbing.

He stepped in and stopped short, expecting to see Sara.

"Where is Sara?" he asked.

"I thought she was with you," his mother said with surprise.

Matthew's heart began to race.

"Could she be resting?" his father asked.

His mother rose. "I will go find out."

Matthew put up a hand. "No, I will go." He ignored her protest and hurried out the door, taking the stairs two at a time.

The word "disappear" played over and over in his mind. Surely, she had not disappeared. Surely not! Not after she had promised.

He knocked on her door.

"Sara!" he called. "Sara! Are you in there?"

If she was resting, he would feel very foolish, but he simply could not wait to find out. He turned to see that his mother had arrived at his elbow.

"Stop shouting, Matthew," she whispered. "The servants will hear you, and if Sara is sleeping, she will not welcome such a commotion. What has come over you?"

Ignoring his mother, he banged on the door before reaching for the knob.

"Matthew!" she remonstrated. "Let me." She opened the door and peeked in.

"Sara, my dear?" she whispered. "Are you sleeping?"

Matthew pushed the door wide and looked over her shoulder. The room was empty. His mother stepped in and looked into the bathroom. She returned to the door with a shake of her head.

"She is not here. Where could she have gone? I thought she was with you and Emily."

"We dropped her off at the door, and then Emily and I took a drive. I needed to talk to Emily to discover her intentions."

"Her intentions? Do you mean regarding the proposal?"

His mother hurried after him as he retreated down the hall and ran down the stairs.

"Perhaps Sara is in the garden?" his mother said.

"Yes, the proposal," he threw over his shoulder. He ran out the back door and stood on the porch.

"Sara!" he called.

"Matthew! Do not stand out here and shout for her like a banshee. You will frighten her."

He could not deny the feeling of dread that seized his heart. Sara had disappeared. She had vanished as she had done before.

He shook his head.

"No, Mother. She is gone. She has disappeared. She did this once before, and I did not know what happened to her. She promised me she would not do this again!"

Matthew's father had joined them on the back porch.

"What is all the shouting about? Are you still looking for Sara?"

Matthew stared into the garden without seeing it. He heard his mother speak.

"Yes, she seems to have disappeared. She is not in her room, nor in the garden."

"Well, perhaps she went for a walk," his father said sensibly, "although I would not have recommended that she do so." He checked his pocket watch. "It is already four o'clock. It will be dark soon."

Matthew swung around. "That is it! She said something about a walk, and I told her that it was not safe. She *would* do something foolish like that. She does things like that."

He rushed past his parents and out the front door of the house. Craning his neck, he stared at the road leading down the hill but could not see Sara.

He jumped down from the front steps and ran out into the drive.

"Take the carriage, boy," his father called out. "You cannot chase her on foot. You have no idea where she has gone!"

Matthew scanned the road ahead and turned back with reluctance to see his parents and Mrs. Roe standing just outside the front door. His father turned and spoke to Mrs. Roe, who hurried away.

"I've ordered the carriage," his father said. "I suggest you circle each block. She may have gotten herself lost."

"Yes, thank you, Father. I will," Matthew said. While his parents watched helplessly, Matthew paced the front steps, waiting for Raymond to bring the carriage around.

He consulted his watch, but only a few moments had passed since his father stated it was four o'clock. Yet the late afternoon sky seemed to have darkened considerably over that short period of time.

"I must find her," he muttered to no one in particular.

"You will, Matthew," his mother said.

His parents could not know that his deepest fear was that Sara had voluntarily disappeared. He could not share that fear with them. To do so would be to raise myriad questions, and perhaps even the suggestion that he simply let her go if she wished to vanish, especially if she had done so once before.

But he could not let her go! He simply could not! He loved her. He could not lose her.

Raymond brought the carriage around.

"Make haste, Raymond. I will direct you," Matthew said as he jumped up into the box beside the driver.

"We are looking for Miss Reed, Raymond," Matthew said hastily as they sped away from the house. "Keep a sharp eye out."

They trotted down the hill without sight of her, circling each block slowly, but to no avail. Matthew stopped short of calling for her, not wishing to draw attention to himself or her.

Darkness came quickly, and when they could no longer see anything but the horses' heads, Matthew directed Raymond to turn for home.

He stepped down from the carriage and paused on the front steps until Raymond pulled away to return the carriage to the stable at the back of the house. Matthew turned to look down over the lights of the city and those twinkling from ships in the bay.

Where could Sara have gone? And why? Why had she left? She had promised him she would not disappear. Yet she had. He shoved his cold hands in his coat pockets. His heart felt as cold as his hands.

That was it then. Sara was gone. He had no hope of finding her in such a large city. None at all. Nor would searching for her be a wise thing. Sara had left the house voluntarily, and to hound her was unpardonable. He could not in all conscience do so.

CHAPTER TWENTY-TWO

Sara pried one eye open then the other. A sliver of daylight filtered in through a crack in dark curtains. She tried to lift her head, but the effort seemed too much. The room spun, if it was indeed a room.

A sharp pain from her ankle shot into her foot, and she gasped and reached for her knee, trying to pull her leg to her chest. The movement made her nauseous, and she stopped moving, closing her eyes for a moment while the dizziness passed.

Where on earth was she? The room, though dimly lit, appeared to be a bedroom, but it wasn't her bedroom at the Webster house. She heard the faint jingle of horse livery outside the window.

She tried lifting her head again, but the nausea returned.

"Hello?" she whispered. She wasn't really sure she wanted anyone to come, but then again, she had to ask someone where she was.

There was no answer. She scanned the room as best she could. She lay on a bed, with a light-colored quilt drawn up to her chin. The pillow beneath her head was soft, the casing a soft linen. A nightstand by the bed held a lamp, a glass of water, a small dark bottle and a spoon. She reached for the bottle but couldn't read it in the muted light. She set it back on the nightstand.

A wardrobe, a dressing table and several small chairs completed the room.

"Hello?" she called out, a little more loudly this time. No answer.

She tried pushing herself up on her elbow. She appeared to be wearing some sort of white soft cotton nightgown. Where were her clothes?

Sara's pulse quickened, albeit sluggishly. Where was she and who had taken her clothes?

"Joseph Conrad," she murmured. That was the name of the man who had picked her up from the street. She must have fainted, because that was the last memory she had.

Another look down at her nightgown prompted her to jerk her head to the right and look over her shoulder. No! She was alone in the small bed. Thank goodness!

Fighting the dizziness, she pushed back the covers and lowered her legs. Her right ankle pulsated with pain, and she gasped, wanting nothing more than to drop back onto the bed and faint. She had to get to the window though to find out where she was. She noted her ankle was wrapped in a bandage. The nightgown she wore, obviously made for a taller woman, swept the floor

Sara lowered her good foot to the ground and balanced herself against the nightstand. She managed to hop over to the window by grabbing onto furniture as she moved. Dizziness almost bested her a couple of times, and she waited for it to pass.

She threw herself onto the windowsill, and bracing herself with one hand, she pulled the curtains aside with her free hand to find herself staring through the window glass at a row of tall brick buildings. The street below bustled with wagons, carriages, streetcars and pedestrians. From the looks of things, she was still in nineteen hundred.

She gathered she was in downtown Seattle, but for all she knew, she could have been in a different city or state. She had no idea how long she'd been unconscious or why she felt so nauseous.

Bracing herself with her stomach, she freed her hands and tried to lift the window, but it wouldn't budge...or she didn't know how to work it.

She rotated on her good foot and half sat on the windowsill to survey the room. She would have to make it over to the door but feared what she might find on the other side. Was she in a hospital? An asylum? Had Joseph Conrad actually kidnapped her? Why hadn't he taken her back to the Webster house?

The door opened, and Sara let out a small gasp.

A gray-haired woman peeped in and looked toward the bed. She then looked toward the window where Sara wrapped her arms defensively across her chest.

"Good morning," the woman said on entering. She smiled widely, and Sara relaxed. "How do you feel? You shouldn't be on that ankle, dear. Let me help you back to bed. The doctor said you are to stay off your feet for a week."

The light from the window revealed a middle-aged woman with a friendly face. Blue eyes regarded her kindly. Tall and slender, she must have been the original owner of the nightgown.

Without waiting for Sara's response, the woman half carried Sara back to the bed and helped her into it. Sara's ankle ached from the activity, and she fought back a grunt or two.

"Are you in pain, dear? The doctor left some morphine for you. I don't use the stuff myself, but the doctor said you might need it for the pain." She picked up the bottle and spoon.

"Morphine?" Sara gasped. She shook her head vehemently. "No! I can't take morphine. Oh, no!"

"No? Well, he gave you some last night because you were in such a state."

"I'm nauseous," Sara said.

The woman nodded.

"Yes, it affects me that way too. That's why I don't take it. I'm Edna Conrad, by the way."

"Sara Reed," Sara said.

"My husband, Joseph, found you last night, but he said you fainted before you could tell him your name or where you live."

"I think I did," Sara murmured. She realized for the first time that Matthew probably had no idea where she was. She had, in fact, disappeared, something she promised she wouldn't do.

"I need to get word to the family I'm staying with," she said hastily. "The Websters? Do you know them?"

"The Websters?" Mrs. Conrad shook her head. "I don't think I do. Where do they live?"

"On Queen Anne Hill?"

"Oh, yes, of course, that is where Joseph said he found you. He had been visiting a business associate up there." To Sara's dismay, she shook her head again. "But no, I do not know anyone who lives on Queen Anne Hill."

"Maybe your husband does?" Sara asked.

Mrs. Conrad shook her head. "He had to go down to Portland on business this morning and will be gone for a week. But I don't think he knows anyone named the Websters either."

"They'll worry about me," Sara said, thinking of Matthew specifically.

"I wish I could help you, my dear, but I don't know how. Do you have any family we could contact?"

Sara shook her head. The movement made her queasy again, and she eyed the bottle of morphine with horror.

"No, I don't."

"You look pale, dear. I think you should have something to eat, and we can give the matter further thought when you feel better. I will have my housekeeper bring you some tea and toast."

Sara leaned her head back against the pillows. There was nothing she could do right now. She couldn't pick up a cell phone, and even if she had one, there was no directory assistance to find Matthew's cell phone...even if *he* had one. She didn't know the address of the Webster house and couldn't, at this moment, go wandering the streets of Seattle until she found it.

"Thank you," she sighed.

Mrs. Conrad left the room, and Sara felt hot tears slide down her cheeks. She had broken her word to Matthew. Well, he would think she had broken her word. She hadn't even told anyone she was going for a walk. If she had, Matthew would have at least known that she meant to return.

A plump woman knocked on the door a short while later and maneuvered her way in the door with a silver tray.

"Here you are, miss. Some tea and toast." She set the tray on the bed beside Sara.

"Thank you, Mrs...." Sara lifted an eyebrow.

"Olson, miss. I'm the housekeeper." White fluffy hair crowned a cheerful pink face.

"Thank you, Mrs. Olson." Sara looked at the tray but tried to hide her grimace at the thought of food.

"Eat now, miss. You need your strength." Mrs. Olson poured out a cup of tea and handed it to Sara, apparently intent on waiting to see if Sara drank it. Sara obediently took a sip. It did go down very smoothly.

Mrs. Olson beamed and rubbed her hands on her apron.

"Well, I've got to go help the cook with dinner, so I'll leave you to eat."

"Dinner?" Sara squeaked. "Dinner? What time is it?"

Mrs. Olson checked a small watch pinned to her dark-brown dress.

"Just about three o'clock, miss."

Sara's hand holding the cup shook. "Three o'clock?" she repeated in a whisper. She had been gone about twenty-four hours.

"Yes, miss. You slept a long time—Mrs. Conrad said because of the pain medication the doctor gave you."

Sara nodded, fighting back another round of tears. Her throat ached from the effort. She would have given anything to just run downstairs and trot back to Queen Anne Hill, but her ankle would never have allowed her to make the trip. She supposed she could hire a carriage, but she had no money and no idea where to tell the carriage to go.

Mrs. Olson left, and Sara set down her tea and made the painful and arduous journey back to the window to stare down at the street. What could she do? What must Matthew be thinking?

She stood there on one foot, trying to ignore the pulsing pain in her right ankle, until Mrs. Conrad returned to the room and dragged her back to bed.

"You have not even eaten your toast," she chided. "Well, supper will be ready soon. Mrs. Olson will bring you a nice plate of stew."

"Where are my clothes?" Sara asked, not completely giving up on an idea of trying to make it back to Queen Anne Hill.

"They are being laundered," Mrs. Conrad said. "Joseph said he found you in the road. Your clothes were mired in dirt."

"How long will that take?" Sara said.

Mrs. Conrad smiled. "It is damp today, as it often is here in Seattle. Your things will probably take a few days to dry."

Sara swallowed hard. No, she needed clothes before that.

"Rest now, dear. I will send Mrs. Olson up with supper soon. I hope you have an appetite by then."

Sara knew she wouldn't. The only thing that would give her an appetite was the sight of Matthew standing before her, a warm smile on his face. No, even if he was angry with her, as long as she could see him and explain what had happened. As long as she could see him.

As promised, Mrs. Olson brought stew in a few hours. She turned on the bedside lamp and waited while Sara took a few bites, but when the housekeeper left, Sara dropped her spoon and any pretense of eating. Feeling slightly less dizzy than she had that morning, she pushed off from the bed again and hopped to the window. Night had fallen, the early darkness that came with fall, and she stared down at the street now devoid of the busy commercial wagon traffic she had seen earlier.

Streetlamps lit the road, highlighting the occasional pedestrians who strolled by, perhaps for an after-dinner walk. The now dark and forbidding brick building directly opposite seemed to house a small restaurant on its ground floor.

She tugged at the window again, but it wouldn't budge. She had no idea why she needed to have the window open. The overcoats on the men and women indicated the night air was brisk. She wasn't Rapunzel, who needed to let down her hair to be rescued from her tower. She couldn't very well wander the streets asking if anyone knew of the Websters and where they lived on Queen Anne Hill.

Acutely aware of the needs of nature, Sara hobbled into the connecting bathroom. She washed her face and hands, swatted at her rumpled hair, and returned to the bedroom, her only decision whether to stare out the window again or get back into bed. The persistent throbbing in her ankle told her she probably needed to elevate her foot, so she hopped back to the bed and climbed in.

Mrs. Olson came to get her tray in a bit, and Sara closed her eyes and tried, unsuccessfully, not to think about Matthew. Had he and Emily worked out their differences? How long would he look for her? What would his parents think of her disappearance? How could she possibly return to the twenty-first century? Because if Matthew married Emily, Sara knew she didn't want to stay.

The following morning, Sara awakened to bright light in the room. She had forgotten to close the curtains the night before. Her ankle ached, but it no longer throbbed, at least not upon awakening. However, as soon as she lowered her feet to the floor, the pulsating pain began again.

Her dinner tray of food was gone, and she suspected Mrs. Olson had come in and removed the tray, declining to wake her. The effects of the morphine had put her to sleep again early last night, but the accompanying dizziness and nausea were gone, at least for now.

She crawled out of bed and cruised over to the window using the now familiar path of bracing herself on chairs and the dresser. She had no idea what time it was, but the commercial wagons had appeared again, and a streetcar meandered down the road. Morning rush in downtown Seattle had begun.

Sara leaned her elbows on the sill and watched the activity. Several carriages pulled up to the building across the street and discharged well-groomed men sporting derbies and elegant overcoats. They bypassed the restaurant, which appeared closed, and used the main entrance to the building.

Sara was on the verge of turning away and heading for the bathroom when one such carriage caught her eye. Or rather, the driver caught her eye.

Raymond!

Her heart bounced around in her chest, then began a loud thumping.

Matthew descended from the carriage and paused to talk to Raymond.

Sara yanked at the window, but it still wouldn't open. She resorted to pounding on the window and shouting.

"Matthew! Matthew!"

But Matthew couldn't hear her. He was too far away, and the noise of the street would have deafened her pounding.

Sara didn't wait. She hopped to the door and pulled it open. The room led into a short hallway. She worked her way down the hall, supporting herself along the wall. Coming up to a staircase, she eyed it for a split second before grabbing the rail and bouncing down the stairs.

"I can do this! I can do this!" she muttered with every jarring step. She dragged her injured right foot and smacked the toes on occasion.

"Ouch! Ouch!"

Mrs. Olson appeared at the bottom of the stairs.

"Miss Reed, what are you doing? You shouldn't be out of bed. Mrs. Conrad has gone shopping, but she will be back in a few hours. She would be very unhappy to see you hopping down the stairs like that."

"I have to run across the street," Sara panted. "Out of my way, Mrs. Olson!"

"Across the street?" the housekeeper cried. "In your nightgown?" She shook her head and wrung her hands. "You can't do that, miss."

"Watch me, Mrs. Olson!" Sara hopped to the door and yanked it open. A small level walkway, flanked by a decorative iron rail, led to the street. She eyed the railing some feet from the door and launched herself.

"Miss Reed, not in your nightgown! You're not even wearing any shoes," Mrs. Olson called out.

Sara waved a hand over her head but didn't turn around. She hopped along the railing and balanced herself on one foot at the edge of the road. The brick building on the opposite curb, which had seemed so close, now seemed miles away. Wagons, carriages and a wide dirt street came between her and the building.

Raymond's carriage was no longer there. He must have left. Sara could only hope that he had dropped Matthew off. Surely Matthew hadn't had enough time to do whatever he needed to do in the building?

Sara had no idea how she was supposed to get across the road without anything to hang on to. By now, she was aware that several pedestrians stared at her, and some drivers of wagons looked down at her with odd expressions.

"Miss! Where are you going dressed like that?"

Sara turned to see a policeman approaching. Robust, middle aged with a large handlebar mustache, the uniformed man packing a nightstick shook his head vigorously.

No! No! This couldn't be happening. Surely she wasn't about to be arrested for standing outside in her jammies?

She looked over her shoulder to see Mrs. Olson running down the walk with a blanket in her hands.

"Officer, officer," Mrs. Olson said. "Miss Reed is staying with us."

"Well, she can't be out here dressed like that," he said.

"I have to get to that building," Sara said doggedly. "I have to."

"No, miss, you need to come inside," Mrs. Olson said. She draped the dark-green blanket over Sara's shoulders.

"No!" Sara barked. "Matthew Webster is in there! I need to talk to him."

"In that office building?" the policeman asked. "No, I don't think you

have any business over there today." He turned to Mrs. Olson. "Is she..."
He pointed to his head.

"No, of course not. She has had a foot injury and was in bed," Mrs.
Olson said irritably. "Miss Reed, you have to come inside now."

"She's right, miss. If you don't, I'm going to arrest you for public
indecency."

Sara looked down at the cotton nightgown that trailed in the dirt.

"In this thing? It covers everything. Let me just run across the street,
you guys! This is nuts!"

Mrs. Olson tugged the blanket across Sara's chest.

"This is your last warning, miss. I take you in if you don't go inside!"

Sara launched herself forward, trying to use the toes of her right foot.
She fell flat on her face. The blanket fell to the side.

"That's it then! If you can't control her, lady, I will!"

He pulled Sara up like a rag doll and threw her over his shoulder. She
kicked with her good foot and shrieked.

"Let me down! Let me down!"

From her awkward angle, she lifted her head to see Mrs. Olson
wringing her hands and crying.

"Please don't take her," Mrs. Olson called to the policeman's back.

The policeman ignored them both and carted Sara down the street.

"Mrs. Olson," Sara shouted. "The building across the street. Find
Matthew Webster!

"Put me down!" she barked. She kicked and was rewarded with a
smack on her rear end.

"Stop that, lady!"

They stopped in front of a small boxy dark carriage, and the
policeman stuffed her inside. Out of the corner of her eye, she saw
another policeman holding the reins.

"Where are you taking me?" she shouted, banging on the roof of the
windowless carriage. She tried the doors, but they were locked from the
outside.

No one answered. The carriage moved forward, and Sara grabbed the
strap. She twisted her body and lifted her throbbing ankle onto the bench
seat. Her predicament was only now dawning on her.

She was being arrested...again, and in her nightgown. She was going
to jail in her nightgown with no shoes, no coat, no identification. She
only hoped Mrs. Olson found someone to help her.

The drive didn't take long, and they stopped in about fifteen minutes.
The door opened, and Sara shrank back against the far corner of the
coach. The policeman pulled her out and set her on her feet.

At her cry, he looked down.

"Still hurts, huh?" He lifted her over his shoulder again and carried her up a steep flight of stairs. He entered a large room and dropped her none too gently on a wooden bench in front of a counter.

"Don't move," the policeman said with an admonishing finger as he stepped forward to talk to another officer at the counter.

Nothing in Sara's experience in the Kalispell jail prepared her for the flurry of activity and bustle of the Seattle jail. Five or six men and two other women shared the bench beside her, though all appeared to be fully dressed in day clothes. Sara self-consciously pulled her nightgown closer about her and tucked her now filthy feet under the hem.

"Well, that's one way of advertising your goods, dearie," one of the women, a buxom, middle-aged blonde, said.

Sara turned away. She hadn't thought anything would be worse than the Kalispell jail, but she was mistaken.

"You should try it sometime, Aggie," a skinny, elderly man sitting next to her said. He snorted and cackled. "Some of the rags you've been wearing wouldn't attract a mule, much less a man."

"Well, I'm going to guess she got arrested for walking around in her nightgown, Bert, so maybe that wasn't such a good idea after all." She elbowed him and giggled.

Sara assumed the woman was a prostitute, although from the clothing she wore, Sara wouldn't have suspected. Dressed not in a bright-red satin saloon costume with low cleavage, Aggie wore a filthy white blouse, grayish sweater and plain brown skirt.

Sara looked up to see the policeman pointing to her. Surely they were going to let her go. Public indecency? Please!

To Sara's dismay, a stocky lady, dressed in the dark-blue uniform of the police, albeit with a long skirt instead of trousers, came forward and pulled her to her feet. Sara tried to balance on her one good foot but swayed.

"What's the matter? Have you hurt your foot?" She bent and lifted the hem of Sara's nightgown to look at the bandage. With an expression of exasperation, she turned and spoke to the policeman.

"Ernie, you didn't tell me she was injured."

"Oh, yeah, some kind of foot injury," he said, almost as if he'd forgotten all about Sara.

"Well, I see that now."

She turned back to Sara.

"Come on, I'll help you down to a cell. Hopefully, a family member will come to bail you out fairly quickly, because I don't think you really belong here, young lady."

"I was on the street in my nightgown," Sara said needlessly. She leaned on the woman and hobbled down the hall.

"That's what I heard," she said. "I'm Matron Miller."

The kindly matron toted her out of the booking area and down a steep flight of stairs to a basement area. The smell of sewage immediately assaulted Sara's nose, and she cupped her hand to cover her face.

"They call this the Black Hole, and now you know why," the matron said in a dry voice.

She dragged a reluctant Sara past a row of cells holding crying, moaning and cursing men until they reached what must have been the women's section. Dampness permeated the basement, and mold crawled down the walls.

"Oh, please don't put me in here," Sara cried. "Please don't." Had she known this would be the result of running around in the street in her nightgown, she never would have done it. She would have sent Mrs. Olson to find Matthew.

Matron Miller opened a cell door and gently stuffed Sara inside.

"Hush now! You'll see the judge in a few days unless someone comes to pay your fine. I sincerely hope you have family though. A few days in here can be a death sentence."

With a shake of her head, the matron clanked the door shut and walked away, keys jingling at her waist.

Something warm, furry and fast ran across Sara's feet, and she screamed.

CHAPTER TWENTY-THREE

Matthew tried to sign the documents that needed his immediate attention, but all he could do was brace his forehead in his palms as he sat at his desk.

He could not fathom why Sara would leave, especially when she had promised she would not. Yet, there was so much about her that he did not know. Did she have family in Seattle? Friends? Someone who would take her in? Had she lied to him all along? To what end? She had been on the train to Chicago, not Seattle. Where could she have gone?

A query to the police earlier that morning had elicited nothing. They had never heard of Sara Reed.

The shrill sound of a woman's voice outside his office roused him from his reverie, and he rose from his desk with irritation. Given his sleeplessness the preceding night, he had little patience.

"Charles," he barked as he pulled his office door open. "What is going on?"

His secretary, a slender young man of twenty-two, pushed his glasses back onto his nose and spoke hastily.

"Sir, this woman insists on seeing you."

Matthew regarded the woman—a servant, from the standard gray uniform dress and white apron that she wore. Her plump anxious face was blotched with tears.

"Yes, madam. What can I do for you?"

"Mr. Matthew Webster?" she cried out.

"Yes, madam?"

"I'm Mrs. Olson. I'm the housekeeper for the Conrad family just across the street." Her words came out in a hasty jumble.

"Yes?" Matthew tried to curb his irritation at the intrusion into his reverie.

"Miss Sara Reed. She's been taken to jail!"

"What?" Matthew ran out of his office and grabbed the woman by the arms. "What?"

"Mr. Webster, you're hurting me!"

Matthew unhanded her. "Forgive me, Mrs. Olson. Where is Miss Reed? What happened?"

"She's been taken to jail."

Matthew noted his secretary watching them both with rounded eyes.

"Come with me, Mrs. Olson. Tell me everything."

More gently this time, Matthew took the housekeeper by the arm and led her from his offices down the stairs and out into the street.

"How did this happen? When?" he asked hurriedly.

"Just now," she said. "Only a few minutes ago. They took her away in a paddy wagon."

"Why? Where has she been?"

"She was out in the street in her nightgown," Mrs. Olson said, tears slipping down her face. "I told her she couldn't go out like that, but she didn't seem to understand why. I think she was trying to get to your building."

"Her nightgown? What on earth?" He searched the street for a hired carriage, regretting that he had told Raymond to pick him up in an hour.

He flagged down a carriage.

"She hurt her ankle. Not knowing who she was or where she lived, Mr. Conrad brought her home last night. That is our house, right across the street." She pointed to a brownstone.

"She hurt her ankle?" Matthew cursed himself. She must have gone for a walk and hurt herself.

The carriage stopped, and Matthew shouted the direction to the driver before jumping in.

"Thank you, Mrs. Olson. Thank you!"

"Please get her out, Mr. Webster!"

"I will, Mrs. Olson," he called out.

A short fifteen minutes later, they arrived at city hall, and Matthew told the carriage drive to await him.

He stepped inside and followed the directions to the jail, where he presented himself to the counter.

"Yes?" a police officer asked.

"I am here to pick up Miss Sara Reed. I understand she was erroneously arrested only a short while ago."

"Erroneously?" the short, stocky policeman asked with a lift of his eyebrow.

"Yes," Matthew said firmly.

"I doubt that." Nevertheless, he consulted a ledger. "Yes, a matron just took her downstairs to the cells. Says here she was arrested for public indecency."

Matthew stiffened and turned to survey those within hearing distance. The motley crew sitting on the bench worried him not at all.

"Utter nonsense! What do I need to do to get Miss Reed out of jail?"

"Well, if a fine had been set, you could pay that, but until a judge reviews the case, we won't know what that will be. You could check back on Monday."

Three days? No!

"Who is the judge?"

"Judge Clemson Wilson?"

"Please give me some paper. I wish to send a note to the judge."

"We don't send notes to the judge, mister."

"You will, or Judge Wilson will want to know why you did not."

The policeman narrowed his eyes and stared at Matthew before handing him paper and a pen.

Matthew jotted a note off to the judge, a friend of the family.

"Send the note. I will wait here."

The policeman took the note and handed it to a young policeman, who nodded and left the jail.

Matthew looked at the bench with hesitation but took a seat between a buxom woman and a scrawny man.

"Hello, dearie, what are you in for?" the woman asked, fixing him with a broad, mostly toothless grin.

"I am just waiting," he said. He faced forward. How could Sara possibly have ended up in such a place? He had heard tales of Seattle's jail, often referred to as the Black Hole given its reputation for vermin infestation, disease, filth, sewage, dampness and mold. He prayed Judge Wilson would respond soon.

"Well, I was just waiting for someone like you," she cackled with an elbow in his ribs.

Matthew deduced the woman was a prostitute, albeit an aging one.

"Hey, are you trying to take my girl?" the man to his left squawked, followed by a weak guffaw as he leaned over Matthew to eye the woman with a wink.

Matthew wished himself anywhere but here.

"Not at all," he said politely.

"Aggie, are you cheating on me?" the man continued to laugh, his breath foul.

A short, sturdy woman in uniform approached the bench and hauled

Aggie to her feet.

"Come on, Aggie. I guess you're not going to jail this time. Out you go."

"Thanks, matron! See you later, Carl!"

Carl, the scrawny man to Matthew's left, waved a hand.

"I'll see you on the streets, Aggie!"

The matron gently pushed the woman out of the jail door. With a wipe of her hands, she turned and regarded Matthew.

"Please tell me you're here to get Miss Reed."

Matthew jumped up.

"Yes! Is she all right?"

The matron shook her head.

"Not really. I hated to take her down to the basement. I hear they won't set a fine until Monday at the earliest though."

"I've sent a note to the judge. He is a family friend."

"How could you let her get picked up like that?" she asked with a disapproving frown and pursed lips.

Matthew thought of making excuses, but he resisted.

"I did not watch her closely enough. It is my fault."

"She seems like a nice young woman. Let's hope the judge gets your note."

She shook her head, and to Matthew's dismay, she disappeared out the door. Matthew wanted to keep her in view as he felt certain that she would be the person to bring Sara out of the jail.

An hour passed, and in that period of time, Matthew rose impatiently to pace just outside the booking room several times before returning to reclaim his seat. He watched various prisoners being booked and taken away.

An hour of Sara sitting in the disease-ridden jail. Intolerable.

He rose and approached the policeman at the counter.

"Did the judge receive my note?"

The policeman sighed and turned.

"Jimmy?" he called out.

The young man who had taken the message hurried forward.

"Was the judge upstairs when you took the note?"

He shook his head.

"No, sir, but I left it with his clerk."

"Is the judge in town? Is he at work today?" Matthew asked.

The young man nodded. "Yes, the clerk said he would be back in an hour."

"Thank you," Matthew said. He retook his seat and checked his watch. Almost 5:30 p.m. He knew it would have grown dark outside,

148

with a correlating drop in temperature. He could feel the chill even inside the city hall building.

He did not care to think how cold Sara was in her cell, which he suspected was unheated. Even if the jail provided blankets, they would no doubt be thin and probably dirty. He rose and paced again.

A well-dressed young man entered the jail and surveyed the booking room with some distaste. He held several envelopes in his hand.

"Mr. Webster?" he asked.

Matthew swung to face him.

"Yes?"

"I am Daniel McAllister, Judge Wilson's clerk. Here is a note for you. Miss Reed is to be released with no charges."

"Thank you!" Matthew said. "Tell the judge thank you!"

"Certainly." Young Mr. McAllister handed the other envelope to the policeman on duty, who read it and signaled to Jimmy.

"Go get matron and have her bring Miss Reed up."

Matthew opened his note.

Matthew, my boy!

Good to hear from you. Yes, of course, we will have Miss Reed released at once. I cannot imagine what they were thinking to arrest her in the first place. Utter foolishness!

Remember me to your mother and father.

Yours,

Clemson Wilson

Matthew stuck the note in his overcoat and paced anxiously. Within fifteen minutes, the matron returned, her arm under a filthy, pale and hobbling Sara.

"Thank you," Matthew told the matron. "Sara," he murmured as he swept her cold and shaking body up into his arms and hurried out of the jail.

Sara wrapped her arms around his neck and began to cry.

"I'm sorry," she sobbed. "I went for a walk, then I disappeared. I'm sorry. They had me on morphine. I didn't know the address of the house. No one did."

He made soothing noises as he moved toward the carriage. He lifted her inside the carriage and called out his address to the driver before joining her.

Matthew ignored all notions of propriety and gathered Sara into his arms, pulling her onto his lap. She shuddered with cold, and he wrapped his arms tightly around her.

"It is all right," he whispered. "Everything will be all right now. We will get you home and warmed up."

"What will your parents say when they find out I've been in jail...again?"

"Please do not worry about that, Sara."

"But I do," she cried.

"Yes, I know," he said in a soothing voice.

"And I worry about what you think of me. I must stink."

"Not to me," he said, breathing in the scent of her hair. "Not to me."

"I'm sorry," she said in a hoarse voice, burying her face in his neck. "I'm sorry to be so much trouble."

"Do not be. You are not trouble. These things just seem to happen to you. I cannot bear to hear your apologies for the rest of our lives."

She stilled, and he held her even more tightly.

"The rest of our lives?"

"Yes, the rest of our lives. I love you. I still know so little about you, but I know I cannot bear to lose you. Will you marry me, Sara Reed?"

She stiffened, but he would not loosen his hold on her. Her body was still cold, and she continued to shiver.

"You're right," she whispered near his ear. "You don't know a lot about me, and you should before you decide you love me and want to spend the rest of your life with me."

He turned and kissed her. Her lips, cold at first, warmed under his. He lifted his head and stared into her tear-soaked eyes.

"You will tell me someday. But until then, know that nothing you can say will change my love for you. You have brought chaos and uncertainty and joy into my staid life. I would not have it any other way."

"What about Emily?"

"I cannot marry Emily. I love you."

"I love you, too, Matthew," Sara whispered as she pressed her lips to his. "I feel like I've fallen in time to fall in love with you."

Matthew considered her cryptic words for a moment before succumbing to the sweetness of her kiss. He would ask her the meaning another day, but not this day.

EPILOGUE

Sara heard the toot of a car horn, and she turned from watching the kids play to look out the window. Matthew pulled up in front of the house and jumped out of the car. His pride and joy, the topless bright-red 1903 Packard Model F could only be driven on pleasant days, and this was one of them.

He had called on the telephone to say that he was leaving work early and taking them for a ride. Sara still struggled to understand the mechanics of the phone, but she managed.

She turned as he entered the drawing room, or what she referred to as the living room. Matthew no longer found her expressions strange, and he valued her input on new and modern inventions.

Rather than entrap Matthew into marriage without full knowledge of her origins, Sara had described—soon after he had rescued her from her second jail stay—her cryptic statement regarding falling through time.

At first, she worried that he thought her slightly crazy...or himself. He had shaken his head and stared at her as if he'd never seen her before. She had waited and watched the emotions cross his face—confusion, disbelief, more confusion, thoughtfulness, love and finally a tentative form of acceptance.

"I am not saying that I disbelieve you, my love, because I trust you implicitly, but you can appreciate how hard your story is to comprehend."

She had nodded and said nothing, waiting for him to process the concept of her travel through time.

"It would explain so many of the things that I could not understand about you, the secrets I felt you withheld."

She nodded again, her hands clasped tightly in her lap.

"Your odd appearance in my compartment, your long johns, your unfamiliarity with customs, food and even language. I knew that residency in Spokane could not account for such a vast difference in experience."

She grimaced with embarrassment and nodded.

"I know. Poor Spokane. Some of the stuff I attributed to that city was ridiculous."

He shook his head. "You were desperate to give me answers to my incessant questions."

"Not incessant."

"They must have seemed so. You probably felt trapped at times, wishing yourself well away from my curiosity." His cheeks bronzed, and she lifted a hand and caressed the side of his face.

"No, Matthew, never from you. I never wished myself away from you."

He pulled her hand to his mouth and kissed the palm. Her heart pounded as it always did when Matthew kissed her.

"I loved you," Sara said. "I think I fell in love with you almost as soon as I met you. I didn't want to frighten you with my story, to see you turn away from me."

"I could never turn away from you," Matthew said. "It was not possible then, and it is not possible now. No matter where you come from, you are the love of my life."

A lump formed in Sara's throat. "I hope we have lots of children," she said. A flush spread to her cheeks.

"A large family," he agreed. "And I shall be there as their father, and you their mother."

He knew her well. In some strange way, he had always known her. Maybe she had been born in the wrong time. Maybe time had corrected an error and sent her back to fall in love.

Now, three years later, they had two children and were on their way to a third. Matthew was a wonderful, caring, loving father, and she couldn't have been happier.

Emily had surprised them all and fallen madly in love with the Greenwoods' young Irish nephew, whom she met at her parents' dinner and dance the evening Sara had disappeared. Following their swift wedding, Emily had moved away to her new husband's estate in Ireland, and she wrote that she had two children and was very, very happy.

Mrs. Webster had encountered Mrs. Feeney at the Williamses' dinner and dance, and she had given that poor woman a verbal lashing when she heard Mrs. Feeney gossiping about Sara. Mrs. Feeney, faced with the wrath of a leading matron of society, soon changed her tune and begged

Mrs. Webster's forgiveness. She returned to Kalispell shortly thereafter, and they had not heard of or from her since.

Matthew entered the house and pulled Sara into his arms, humming to a tune as he twirled her around in a circle, to the children's delight and handclaps. Having made her a promise a long time ago that he would dance with her, he never failed to take her into his arms— to make up for the night they should have first danced together, the night she disappeared for the last time.

And she fell in love with him all over again.

ABOUT THE AUTHOR

I began my first fiction-writing attempt when I was fourteen when I shut myself up in my bedroom one summer and obsessively worked on a time travel/pirate novel set in the beloved Caribbean of my youth. Unfortunately, I wasn't able to hammer it out on a manual typewriter (oh yeah, I'm that old) before it was time to go back to school. The draft of that novel has long since disappeared, but the story still simmers within, and I will finish it one day soon.

I was born in Aruba to American parents and lived in Venezuela until my family returned to the United States when I was twelve. I couldn't fight the global travel bug, and I joined the U.S. Air Force at eighteen to "see the world." After twenty-one wonderful and fulfilling years traveling the world and the birth of one beautiful daughter, I pursued my dream of finally getting a college education. With a license in mental health therapy, I worked with veterans. I continue to travel, my first love, and almost all of my books involve travel.

Please visit my website at www.BessMcBride.com. You may also sign up for my newsletter on my web site.

Many of you know I also write a series of short cozy mysteries under the pen name of Minnie Crockwell. Feel free to stop by my web site and learn more about the series at http://www.minniecrockwell.com/books.html

CPSIA information can be obtained at www.ICGtesting.com
Printed in the USA
BVOW04s1300150516

448140BV00016B/366/P